Paul Laurence Dunbar (1872–1906) is acknowledged as the first important black poet in American literature. The author of several books of poetry, four books of short stories, four novels, and one drama, he was born in Dayton, Ohio, to Matilda, a former slave, and Joshua Dunbar, who had escaped from slavery and served in the Civil War. After his parents separated, his mother was left on her own, living in extreme poverty and making a living as a washerwoman. Dunbar graduated from high school in 1891. The only African-American in his class, he became class president and wrote the class poem. After graduating, he took a job as an elevator operator in Dayton's Callahan Building. In 1892, at the age of twenty, he published his first book of poetry, *Oak and Ivy*. His second book of verse, *Majors and Minors*, caught the attention of the famous literary critic William Dean Howells, and Howells's favorable review in *Harper's Weekly* made Dunbar a national figure almost overnight. In 1898, he married Alice Ruth Moore, a teacher and writer from New Orleans. They separated in 1902, the same year Dunbar developed tuberculosis.

William L. Andrews is Senior Associate Dean for the Fine Arts and Humanities at the University of North Carolina at Chapel Hill. He is the author of *The Literary Career of Charles W. Chesnutt* (1980) and *To Tell a Free Story: The First Century of Afro-American Autobiography, 1760–1865* (1986). He is coeditor of *The Norton Anthology of African-American Literature* (1997) and *The Oxford Companion to African-American Literature* (1997).

THE SPORT OF
THE GODS

Paul Laurence Dunbar

With an Introduction by
William L. Andrews

SIGNET CLASSICS

SIGNET CLASSICS
Published by New American Library, a division of
Penguin Group (USA) Inc., 375 Hudson Street,
New York, New York 10014, USA
Penguin Group (Canada), 90 Eglinton Avenue East, Suite 700, Toronto,
Ontario M4P 2Y3, Canada (a division of Pearson Penguin Canada Inc.)
Penguin Books Ltd., 80 Strand, London WC2R 0RL, England
Penguin Ireland, 25 St. Stephen's Green, Dublin 2,
Ireland (a division of Penguin Books Ltd.)
Penguin Group (Australia), 250 Camberwell Road, Camberwell, Victoria 3124,
Australia (a division of Pearson Australia Group Pty. Ltd.)
Penguin Books India Pvt. Ltd., 11 Community Centre, Panchsheel Park,
New Delhi - 110 017, India
Penguin Group (NZ), 67 Apollo Drive, Rosedale, North Shore 0632,
New Zealand (a division of Pearson New Zealand Ltd.)
Penguin Books (South Africa) (Pty.) Ltd., 24 Sturdee Avenue,
Rosebank, Johannesburg 2196, South Africa

Penguin Books Ltd., Registered Offices:
80 Strand, London WC2R 0RL, England

Published by Signet Classics, an imprint of New American Library, a division of
Penguin Group (USA) Inc. Previously published in the Mentor collection *The
African-American Novel in the Age of Reflection*, edited by William L. Andrews

First Signet Classics Printing, December 1999
First Signet Classics Printing (Updated Edition), February 2011
10 9 8 7 6 5 4 3 2

Introduction copyright © William L. Andrews, 1999
All rights reserved

Ⓒ REGISTERED TRADEMARK — MARCA REGISTRADA

Printed in the United States of America

Contents

Introduction   vii

1. The Hamiltons   1

2. A Farewell Dinner   5

3. The Theft   12

4. From a Clear Sky   19

5. The Justice of Men   27

6. Outcasts   36

7. In New York   45

8. An Evening Out   54

9. His Heart's Desire   61

10. A Visitor from Home   72

11. Broken Hopes   80

12. "All the World's a Stage"   90

13. The Oakleys   100

14. Frankenstein   111

15. "Dear, Damned, Delightful Town" 118

16. Skaggs's Theory 123

17. A Yellow Journal 132

18. What Berry Found 139

Selected Bibliography 145

Introduction

Paul Laurence Dunbar was a dying man when he wrote *The Sport of the Gods* in early 1901. After pneumonia threatened his life in March 1899, he contracted tuberculosis, which caused him severe coughing spells and recurring hemorrhages that often left him too exhausted for work. Yet he was a self-supporting author, the most popular literary figure black America had ever produced and one of the most famous American writers of his time. His poems, fiction, and journalism were in demand, and Dunbar, who supported a wife and a mother in comfortable middle-class affluence, could not afford the luxury of invalidism. When one of the better-paying magazines of the day, *Lippincott's,* requested a novel from him in the winter of 1901, Dunbar readily obliged. In a letter he spoke of writing this novel as simply "filling an order for a prose composition" for *Lippincott's.* "I wrote fifty thousand words in thirty days," Dunbar remarked, "but I have never recovered from the strain of it." The result of this toil was *The Sport of the Gods.* It appeared in *Lippincott's* in the spring of 1901; a year later it was published in the United States by Dodd, Mead and Company, the publisher of Dunbar's three previous novels; and in 1903 it came out in England as *The Jest of Fate*. It was the last novel Dunbar wrote. Yet despite its hasty composition, *The Sport of the Gods* has been hailed by critics as the first African-American "great migration" novel, the first foray into naturalism by an African-American writer, and the first treatment of a blues figure in the African-American novel. Whether because of its pioneering themes and iconoclasm or because of its inconsistencies of tone and conflicting purposes, *The Sport of the Gods* never garnered significant praise during its author's short lifetime. But as a revisionary experiment, albeit rushed and unsteady, *The Sport of the Gods* set a bold and independent example for the African-American novel as it entered the modern era.

The final bleak lines of *The Sport of the Gods* (1902)— "they knew they were powerless against some Will infinitely stronger than their own"—link Dunbar's book to the grim realism of such path-breaking naturalist novels as Frank Norris's *McTeague* (1899) and Theodore Dreiser's *Sister Carrie* (1900), in which the lives of the title characters are largely determined by biological, social, and economic forces. Naturalism's honest portrayal of the human condition as one of struggle against an indifferent or hostile environment had an appeal to African-American writers of Dunbar's era, but the tendency of naturalism to minimize or dismiss individual will and human reason as effective means of changing one's environment or fate has always made naturalism problematic for writers and readers of African-American fiction. The degree to which Dunbar wanted *The Sport of the Gods* to be a naturalist novel is debatable, but to the degree that it is such a text, it stands in stark contrast to, if not defiance of, the prevailing mood of the most influential African-American fiction of Dunbar's time.

Frances Ellen Watkins Harper (1825–1911), a stalwart in the antislavery and women's rights movements for a half century, concluded her novel of racial uplift, *Iola Leroy* (1892), with her title character and her husband deciding to leave pleasant prospects in the North to "labor for those who had passed from the old oligarchy of slavery into the new commonwealth of freedom" in the South. Missionaries for Harper's African-American social gospel, Iola and her husband, Dr. Latimer, "a leader in every reform movement for the benefit of the community," return to the South with an optimism and faith clearly endorsed by Harper. In *The Marrow of Tradition* (1901), widely reviewed as a hard-hitting novel of purpose about racial injustice in the South, Charles W. Chesnutt (1858–1932) addressed many of the sociopolitical problems that impelled Harper's heroine and hero on their mission. Having grown up in the South before migrating to the Midwest for the rewards of a successful professional life, Chesnutt knew from personal experience about the power and pervasiveness of racism in the post–Civil War South. Although skeptical about the readiness of Southern whites for reform of their institutions and their racial ideologies, Chesnutt still concluded *The Marrow of Tradition* with an urgent call for action, refusing to believe that change could not be effected if men and women of conscience on both sides of the color line dedicated themselves to the task.

Veering sharply away from the insistence of Harper and Chesnutt on individual moral responsibility for reform, *The Sport of the Gods* severely restricts the role of human agency in effecting meaningful moral or social change. The psychological, social, and economic problems that beset the African-American family whose fortunes Dunbar follows in his last novel do not have a solution, at least none that the characters in the novel or the narrator of the story can articulate. Nothing the characters do, including migration from the South to the North and back again, can reverse the Hamilton family's demoralization or restore it to wholeness. This unflinching analysis of a black family tragedy was gloomy to the point of bitterness. Dunbar must have been aware that such a story was likely to upset black and white readers alike.

African-American autobiography and fiction of the nineteenth century had been outspoken in its portrayal of the threat to black family life represented by slavery and racism before the Civil War and by poverty, ignorance, and white supremacist repression in late-nineteenth-century America. But even the most forceful African-American literary testimony to the distress of the black family— Frank J. Webb's *The Garies and Their Friends* (1857), Harriet Wilson's *Our Nig* (1859), Harriet Jacobs's *Incidents in the Life of a Slave Girl* (1861), and Pauline Hopkins's *Contending Forces* (1900)—proceeded from an implicit belief that individual and societal effort, bolstered by good will and faith, could effect progress. In a world in which human beings, regardless of race, seem to be "the sport of the gods," however, tossed about by an indifferent and arbitrary fate from which there is no escape and no appeal to a God of justice, the idea of progress or of struggle to bring about justice seems futile, if not meaningless. If this is what Dunbar wished to say in *The Sport of the Gods,* then his was a challenge to his readers' social conscience riskier than any African-American fiction writer or any white American writer on race had experimented with before. Decades would pass before African-American writers such as Richard Wright in *Native Son* (1940), William Attaway in *Blood on the Forge* (1941), and Ann Petry in *The Street* (1946) would ask the questions about fate, faith, and progress that Dunbar raised with such devastating results in *The Sport of the Gods.*

If there was one black writer whom most turn-of-the-century American readers would not have considered bleak or despairing, especially about black people's lot in life, it would have been Paul Laurence Dunbar. Dubbed the "Poet Laureate of the Negro race" by Booker T. Washington, Dunbar was best known before the appearance of *The Sport of the Gods* for his lively verse in black dialect, which earned the praise of sophisticated critics and popular readers alike. He also produced a sizable body of fiction, most of it written in a humorous and/or sentimental vein for popular magazines. Although most of his fiction pretends to little more than entertainment, a few stories broach troubling social issues, such as lynching, segregation, the financial bondage of sharecropping, and the exploitation of black workers by organized labor. In a handful of stories, such as "Jimsella" (1898), "The Finish of Patsy Barnes" (1900), and "The Finding of Zach" (1900), Dunbar took his first tentative steps toward exploring the fortunes of Southern black migrants in the North. None of these stories anticipates the grimness and cynicism of *The Sport of the Gods,* however. Although elements of *The Sport of the Gods* were unquestionably influenced by Dunbar's own life, a look at the author's biography does not reveal easy answers as to why he wrote as he did in his last novel.

Paul Laurence Dunbar was born in 1872 in Dayton, Ohio, to former Kentucky plantation slaves who had themselves migrated north: his father Joshua on the

underground railroad before the Civil War, his mother
shortly after the abolition of slavery. Joshua and Matilda
Glass Dunbar's stories of their preemancipation experiences stocked the future writer with much valuable
literary material. Dunbar's parents were divorced when
Paul was young. He grew up under the care of his watch-
ful and encouraging mother. Dunbar was an excellent
and respected student at Dayton high school. The only
African-American in the school, he was elected president of his class and delivered the class's graduation
poem in June 1891. Refused subsequent employment in
Dayton newspaper and legal offices because of his color,
Dunbar found a job as an elevator operator. Between
calls he wrote poems and articles that found publication
in newspapers; he studied his favorite poets: Tennyson,
Shakespeare, Keats, Poe, Longfellow, and the Midwest's
most famous regionalist, James Whitcomb Riley. Late in
1892 a white patron of Dunbar's financed the printing of
Oak and Ivy, the first of more than a half dozen volumes
of poetry Dunbar was to publish in his short literary career. As the demand for his poetry grew and his literary
friendships broadened to include some of the most il-
lustrious writers of his time, Dunbar began a correspon-
dence with Alice Ruth Moore, a black woman poet and
fiction writer from New Orleans, whom he married in
1898. By that time Dunbar had become an internation-
ally acclaimed writer by virtue of the praise for and sales
of his next two collections of poems, *Majors and Minors*
(1896) and *Lyrics of Lowly Life* (1897).

During a triumphal reading tour in Great Britain in
1897 Dunbar went to work on his first novel, *The Uncalled* (1898), which, though a completely told (and
somewhat autobiographical) story of a young man who
refuses to enter the ministry, was coolly reviewed be-

cause of its lack of African-American local color. Simultaneous with his first novel, Dunbar also brought out his first collection of short stories, *Folks from Dixie,* which dealt with black people from both the slavery era and the post-Reconstruction period. Many of the stories in this and three subsequent volumes of Dunbar's short fiction celebrate the simple pleasures of "down home" living for African-Americans, who find fulfillment in their own communities apart from and seemingly unmindful of the world of whites. Only a comparative few of Dunbar's stories offer candid assessments of social problems occasioned by race. Occasionally, however, Dunbar put aside the mask of sentiment, piety, and easy moralizing that he generally wore for the readers of his fiction to disclose doubts about the faith in African-American self-help and community uplift maintained by a Frances Harper or the crusading hope for social reform that a Charles Chesnutt clung to. *The Sport of the Gods* may thus be read as Dunbar's critique of ideals and myths that he as well as Harper and Chesnutt had subscribed to in much of their fiction, particularly the faith in the progressive advancement of African Americans and the idea of the Southern black community as self-sustaining and ultimately triumphant over adversity and injustice.

Did *The Sport of the Gods* signal a turning point in the artistic evolution of Paul Laurence Dunbar? Would the facile humorist have turned increasingly to satire, his sentimentality exchanged for a more tough-minded realism? Unfortunately, too little time and energy remained to Dunbar after *The Sport of the Gods* to give a clear indication of where he might have been headed. A few months before the book publication of *The Sport of the Gods,* the author and his wife separated. Worsening health, exacerbated by heavy drinking, and harried finances gave Dunbar scant opportunity to pursue the directions and implications of his last novel. He died on February 9, 1906, in Dayton.

Like most great African-American fiction, *The Sport of the Gods* is grounded in a concern with major social and economic problems that were facing black America at the time of its publication. The pretext of the novel seems clearly to be the advantages and disadvantages of black migration from the rural South to the urban North. As early as 1879 African-Americans had begun to leave the South in search of better opportunities on the plains of the Midwest. This northbound stream of black population deepened and widened in the 1880s and 1890s as discriminatory legislation across the states of the former Confederacy forced African-Americans either to adjust to cradle-to-grave segregation or move. Black unemployment in the South was high, occasioned by a sagging market for cotton and by restricted opportunities for education and training in skilled trades. Still, when Dunbar wrote *The Sport of the Gods*, ninety percent of the black people in the United States remained in the South, and eighty percent of black Southerners lived in rural areas. The "great migrations" of millions of black people to the North and Midwest did not get into high gear until World War I and the 1920s and 1930s. Thus, while Dunbar may be read as anticipating a social phenomenon of tremendous importance to black America in the twentieth century, his migrants—the Hamilton family—do not fit the profile of the average migrant from the South, most of whom went North because they heard or read about better jobs and, after World War I, attractive black communities in big cities such as New York, Chicago, and Detroit. The Hamiltons leave the

South because they have to, not because they seek better jobs but because they have been more or less banished from their hometown. Though Dunbar may have wanted the Hamiltons' story to serve as a kind of case study of migration, readers should keep in mind that in several respects the Hamiltons do not seem typical of early-twentieth-century black southern migrants. Indeed, for Dunbar's novel to make its full impact, readers must accept Dunbar's definition of what makes the Hamiltons representative and therefore sympathetic.

The older generation of the Hamilton family, Berry and his wife, Fannie, represent the majority of Southern slave-born African-Americans. Enduring rather than trying to escape slavery, they stayed in the South when freedom came. The years after emancipation found them, according to the narrator of *The Sport of the Gods,* "waiting, working, and struggling to rise" in "their own beloved section," the South. The evidence of their successes abounds in the first chapter of *The Sport of the Gods.* Their "neatly furnished, modern house" announces "the home of a typical, good-living Negro." Berry works for his former master as a butler, but his duties do not prevent him from raising a family, joining a fraternal lodge, and enjoying high status in his community. His wife presides over her own home and garden; she does not have to take in laundry or place her pretty teenage daughter, Kitty, in some white family's service to help maintain the family. Joe Hamilton, at eighteen on the threshold of manhood, works in a respectable barbershop, attending to a white clientele, and has enough disposable income to be, in the narrator's words, "a dandy." The Hamilton family, to all appearances, display the complacency of people who are satisfied with the world as it is. At worst self-satisfied and at best naive, these simple, well-meaning people are totally unprepared for the trauma about to befall them.

When the brother of Berry's employer, Maurice Oakley, announces that he has been robbed, the Hamiltons discover just how slight and illusory is the foundation on which they have built their life. Berry's long-standing reputation as "an honest, sensible Negro" dissolves as whites give vent to their racial prejudices and blacks divulge their envy and resentment toward the entire family. Oakley's knee-jerk reaction to the theft of his brother's money is to denounce the most convenient black suspect, Berry Hamilton, on the strength of the white man's conviction that ex-slaves are too ambitious and covetous of what their former masters have. Other former slaveholders of Oakley's cohort ruminate on the general irresponsibility and amorality of black people while approving the verdict of the kangaroo court that sentences Berry Hamilton to ten years in the penitentiary for a crime he steadfastly refuses to confess to. Meanwhile the black community, which knows Berry much better than the bigoted Southern whites and has reason to feel greater empathy in light of his arbitrary racial victimization, turns its collective back on Berry and his family. "If they had sympathy," the narrator of the novel comments, "they dared not show it." The "fear and disloyalty" that cause black people to shun any black person accused by whites of criminal behavior are, according to the narrator, "a heritage from the days of their bondage." In such language Dunbar introduces early into his novel the suggestion that the thinking and behavior of both blacks and whites in the South are strongly influenced by social forces—class consciousness among blacks, racism among whites—that they are either insufficiently aware of (in the case of the spiteful blacks) or (in the case of the bigoted whites) cannot subject to thoughtful analysis. Ultimately, the entire Hamilton family is made to suffer for the supposed transgression of the father.

Fannie, Joe, and Kitty Hamilton move to New York City seeking refuge. It "seemed to them the centre of all the glory, all the wealth, and all the freedom of the world," a place where no one "would look down upon them." The narrator of *The Sport of the Gods* quickly discounts such an elevated view of the city, comparing its effects on "provincials" like the Hamiltons to the intoxication of "insidious wine." The narrator's warnings—to "be wise" and "go away" rather than "be a fool" and "stay on until the town becomes all in all"— echo the moralizing of countless American melodramas of the nineteenth century, which decried the degeneracy of the city and upheld traditional values associated with rural and village life. In his autobiography, *Up From Slavery* (1901), Booker T. Washington, the most prominent African-American at the turn of the century, also lamented the effect of urban conditions on black people. Blacks in the city ended up, Washington claimed, "living by their wits," while black country folk built their lives on a secure agrarian foundation. The careers of Fannie, Joe, and Kitty Hamilton in New York bear out the predictions of degeneration that traditionalists, white and black, often resorted to in observing the growing urbanization of America in the late nineteenth and early twentieth centuries. Joe Hamilton becomes an alcoholic and in a drunken rage commits murder. The tawdry glamor of the dance hall stage becomes the "quick poison" that corrupts Kitty and eventually lures her into the peripatetic, morally compromised life of a chorus girl. Once she leaves her mother to live on her own, her "chief aim was the possession of good clothes and the ability to attract the attention which she had learned to crave." As for Fannie Hamilton, the strain of losing both her children to the lower elements of the city impels her into a bigamous marriage of convenience with an abusive gambler, who too easily convinces her that Berry's prison sentence has put an end to their marriage. Thus all three of the Hamiltons come to moral ruin in the wake of their migration to New York. Their family decimated, none is strong enough on his or her own to stand up to the cynicism, amorality, and exploitativeness of the urban world into which they unwittingly plunge.

The image of black New York that Dunbar purveys in *The Sport of the Gods* is almost entirely negative. The picture is drawn not from Harlem (which lacked even a significant black minority until after Dunbar's death) but rather from the notorious Tenderloin district in lower Manhattan, a magnet to New York City's nonwhites starting in the early nineteenth century. The Tenderloin was a tough part of town, in which cabarets, vaudeville theaters, drinking establishments, and bordellos attracted those who wanted to be part of "the sporting life." The sleazy Banner Club in *The Sport of the Gods,* patterned on clubs that Dunbar learned about during visits to New York in the late 1890s, provides a stage on which much of the downward action in the middle of the novel takes place. Dunbar's attitude toward the Banner Club as "an institution for the lower education of Negro youth," is condemnatory. "Of course, the place was a social cesspool, generating a poisonous miasma and reeking with the stench of decayed and rotten moralities." The "catering cupidity" of the hustlers, parasites, and hangers-on who frequent the club inexorably draws the unwary Joe Hamilton to his doom. Yet the narrator of the novel cannot express sympathy for Joe, "this small-souled, warped being," even though "he was so evidently the jest of Fate." From the outset of his life in New York, Joe is "so blissfully, so conceitedly, unconscious of his own nastiness" that the narrator cannot treat him as anything other than contemptible. Given the fact that this "jest of Fate" had arrived in New York with a head full of "false ideals," "ignorant desires," and "a sort of mental and moral astigmatism that made him see everything wrong," Joe Hamilton would seem to have been almost predetermined for destruction by the forces of the city. Yet at the same time that Dunbar portrays Joe as fated to fail, the narrator also denounces him for his inability to recognize his own failure. One question the novel raises is, what can prevent black migrants to the city from following Joe's miserable example?

The narrator of *The Sport of the Gods* complains often that when rural people like Joe Hamilton come to the urban North they willfully ignore the values they once lived by in the South, embracing instead the debased standards of the city. The narrator celebrates "the old teachings and old traditions" of the South, ridiculing Joe for disregarding them and decrying Kitty's desertion of "the simple old songs" she learned at home in favor of "the detestable coon ditties which the stage demanded" in New York. What the narrator does not make clear in the novel is what exactly "the old teachings" or "the old traditions" are or were, nor does the narrator explain the alternative they represent to. the "false ideals and unreal ambitions" of the city. Instead the novel seems resigned to a weary fatalism about the "sacrifice" of "young Negro life" from the South to "the hard necessities of the city" and the inevitable losing "battle with the terrible force of a strange and unusual environment."

In the final chapter of the novel Dunbar gives Berry and Fannie Hamilton a reprieve from the barrenness of their children's future by allowing them to return to their hometown in the South. But they are powerless to restore their past life. One of the ultimate ironies of the novel is that what motivates the white journalist who delivers Berry from prison and makes possible his reunion with Fannie is not a concern for justice but blatant self-promotion and money-grubbing. If the "gods" who sport with the fates of the Hamiltons consist of racist Southerners like Oakley and pseudo-liberal opportunists in the North like Skaggs, readers of Dunbar's novel have little reason to look to whites for an improvement in the social climate for black people in the North or the South.

After reading _The Sport of the Gods,_ however, one comes away with the feeling that Dunbar found little consolation in the themes of human futility and fatalism that arise from his portrayal of black migration. Unwilling or unable to assume the posture of nonjudgmental detachment favored by the naturalists, Dunbar's novel sometimes betrays a lingering allegiance to the moral idealism of his African-American literary compatriots Harper and Chesnutt. Hence, for instance, the climactic moment of moral self-recognition for Berry Hamilton, when he views the corpse of his wife's second husband and "all his dead faith sprang into new life in a glorious resurrection" of thanksgiving to God for having saved him from murder. Perhaps a desire for an alternative to mere cynicism helps explain the strongly satirical tone that the novelist takes toward so many of his characters, white and black alike. For whatever reason, _The Sport of the Gods_ refuses to resolve itself as either a tragedy (is Joe Hamilton's fall tragic?) or a comedy (does the reunion of Berry and Fannie make for a happy ending?). Instead the novel seems to oscillate between a naturalist study of people caught up in social forces beyond their control and a satirical attack on those same forces and the people who fall victim to them. Possibly Dunbar lacked the novelistic experience or the craftsmanship necessary to fashion this story into either a tragedy or a comedy, a naturalist study or a social satire. But it is also possible that Dunbar intended to create the kind of contradictory text that *The Sport of the Gods* actually is. Maybe Dunbar was trying to propose what we might call a "blues perspective" in which to interpret the fates of the Hamiltons. If the blues response to black experience entails an ability to "laugh to keep from crying" over a perpetual condition of struggle, then the narrator's attitude toward the central figures in *The Sport of the Gods* may very well be associated with the blues. Moreover, the novel itself brings forth a model of blues commentary in the highly self-conscious self-contradictoriness of Sadness, the provocative con man–confidant of the doomed Joe Hamilton. In his wry humor, his disarmingly boastful confessions, his realistic estimate of himself and his world, and his ability to hold in the balance a tragic view of himself as victim and a comic self-estimate of his own failings, Sadness looks well beyond the world view of most nineteenth-century African-American fictional heroes to anticipate the modern consciousness of a Jim Trueblood in Ralph Ellison's *Invisible Man* (1952) or a Shug Avery in Alice Walker's *The Color Purple* (1982). In the unresolved, and seemingly unresolvable, problems that Dunbar posed in *The Sport of the Gods* we may find an incipient call for a new fiction to confront new phenomena—the northern urban ghetto and the consciousness it instilled in black people—in ways that would take African-American fiction beyond the moral categories and accepted literary modes of the nineteenth century and place it in the forefront of the modern American novel.

—William L. Andrews
1999

THE SPORT
OF THE GODS

CHAPTER 1

The Hamiltons

FICTION HAS SAID so much in regret of the old days when there were plantations and overseers and masters and slaves, that it was good to come upon such a household as Berry Hamilton's, if for no other reason than that it afforded a relief from the monotony of tiresome iteration.

The little cottage in which he lived with his wife, Fannie, who was housekeeper to the Oakleys, and his son and daughter, Joe and Kit, sat back in the yard some hundred paces from the mansion of his employer. It was somewhat in the manner of the old cabin in the quarters, with which usage as well as tradition had made both master and servant familiar. But, unlike the cabin of the elder day, it was a neatly furnished, modern house, the home of a typical, good-living negro. For twenty years Berry Hamilton had been butler for Maurice Oakley. He was one of the many slaves who upon their accession to freedom had not left the South, but had wandered from place to place in their own beloved section, waiting, working, and struggling to rise with its rehabilitated fortunes.

The first faint signs of recovery were being seen when

he came to Maurice Oakley as a servant. Through thick and thin he remained with him, and when the final upward tendency of his employer began his fortunes had increased in like manner. When, having married, Oakley bought the great house in which he now lived, he left the little servant's cottage in the yard, for, as he said laughingly, "There is no telling when Berry will be following my example and be taking a wife unto himself."

His joking prophecy came true very soon. Berry had long had a tenderness for Fannie, the housekeeper. As she retained her post under the new Mrs. Oakley, and as there was a cottage ready to his hand, it promised to be cheaper and more convenient all around to get married. Fannie was willing, and so the matter was settled.

Fannie had never regretted her choice, nor had Berry ever had cause to curse his utilitarian ideas. The stream of years had flowed pleasantly and peacefully with them. Their little sorrows had come, but their joys had been many.

As time went on, the little cottage grew in comfort. It was replenished with things handed down from "the house" from time to time and with others bought from the pair's earnings.

Berry had time for his lodge, and Fannie time to spare for her own house and garden. Flowers bloomed in the little plot in front and behind it; vegetables and greens testified to the housewife's industry.

Over the door of the little house a fine Virginia creeper bent and fell in graceful curves, and a cluster of insistent morning-glories clung in summer about its stalwart stock.

It was into this bower of peace and comfort that Joe and Kitty were born. They brought a new sunlight into the house and a new joy to the father's and mother's hearts. Their early lives were pleasant and carefully guarded. They got what schooling the town afforded, but both went to work early, Kitty helping her mother and Joe learning the trade of barber.

Kit was the delight of her mother's life. She was a pretty, cheery little thing, and could sing like a lark. Joe too was of a cheerful disposition, but from scraping the chins of aristocrats came to imbibe some of their ideas, and rather too early in life bid fair to be a dandy. But his father encouraged him, for, said he, "It's de p'opah thing fu' a man what waits on quality to have quality mannahs an' to waih quality clothes."

" 'Tain't no use to be a-humo'in' dat boy too much, Be'y," Fannie had replied, although she did fully as much "humo'in' " as her husband; "hit sho' do mek' him biggety, an' a biggety po' niggah is a 'bomination befo' de face of de Lawd; but I know 'tain't no use a-talkin' to you, fu' you plum boun' up in dat Joe."

Her own eyes would follow the boy lovingly and proudly even as she chided. She could not say very much, either, for Berry always had the reply that she was spoiling Kit out of all reason. The girl did have the prettiest clothes of any of her race in the town, and when she was to sing for the Benefit of the A. M. E. church or for the benefit of her father's society, the Tribe of Benjamin, there was nothing too good for her to wear. In this too they were aided and abetted by Mrs. Oakley, who also took a lively interest in the girl.

So the two doting parents had their chats and their jokes at each other's expense and went bravely on, doing their duties and spoiling their children much as white fathers and mothers are wont to do.

What the less fortunate negroes of the community said of them and their offspring is really not worth while.

Envy has a sharp tongue, and when has not the aristocrat been the target for the plebeian's sneers?

Joe and Kit were respectively eighteen and sixteen at the time when the preparations for Maurice Oakley's farewell dinner to his brother, Francis, were agitating the whole Hamilton household. All of them had a hand in the work: Joe had shaved the two men; Kit had helped Mrs. Oakley's maid; the mother had fretted herself weak over the shortcomings of a cook that had been in the family nearly as long as herself, while Berry was stern and dignified in anticipation of the glorious figure he was to make in serving.

When all was ready, peace again settled upon the Hamiltons. Mrs. Hamilton, in the whitest of white aprons, prepared to be on hand to annoy the cook still more; Kit was ready to station herself where she could view the finery; Joe had condescended to promise to be home in time to eat some of the good things, and Berry—Berry was gorgeous in his evening suit with the white waistcoat, as he directed the nimble waiters hither and thither.

CHAPTER 2

A Farewell Dinner

MAURICE OAKLEY was not a man of sudden or violent enthusiasms. Conservatism was the quality that had been the foundation of his fortunes at a time when the disruption of the country had involved most of the men of his region in ruin.

Without giving any one ground to charge him with being lukewarm or renegade to his cause, he had yet so adroitly managed his affairs that when peace came he was able quickly to recover much of the ground lost during the war. With a rare genius for adapting himself to new conditions, he accepted the changed order of things with a passive resignation, but with a stern determination to make the most out of any good that might be in it.

It was a favorite remark of his that there must be some good in every system, and it was the duty of the citizen to find out that good and make it pay. He had done this. His house, his reputation, his satisfaction, were all evidences that he had succeeded.

A childless man, he bestowed upon his younger brother, Francis, the enthusiasm he would have given to a son. His wife shared with her husband this feeling for her brother-in-law, and with him played the rôle of parent, which had otherwise been denied her.

It was true that Francis Oakley was only a half-brother to Maurice, the son of a second and not too fortunate marriage, but there was no halving of the love which the elder man had given to him from childhood up.

At the first intimation that Francis had artistic ability, his brother had placed him under the best masters in America, and later, when the promise of his youth had begun to blossom, he sent him to Paris, although the expenditure just at that time demanded a sacrifice which might have been the ruin of Maurice's own career. Francis's promise had never come to entire fulfillment. He was always trembling on the verge of a great success without quite plunging into it. Despite the joy which his presence gave his brother and sister-in-law, most of his time was spent abroad, where he could find just the atmosphere that suited his delicate artistic nature. After a visit of two months he was about returning to Paris for a stay of five years. At last he was going to apply himself steadily and try to be less the dilettante.

The company which Maurice Oakley brought together to say good-bye to his brother on this occasion was drawn from the best that this fine old Southern town afforded. There were colonels there at whose titles and the owners' rights to them no one could laugh; there were brilliant women there who had queened it in Richmond, Baltimore, Louisville, and New Orleans, and every Southern capital under the old régime, and there were younger ones there of wit and beauty who were just beginning to hold their court. For Francis was a great favorite both with men and women. He was a handsome man, tall, slender, and graceful. He had the face and brow of a poet, a pallid face framed in a mass of dark hair. There was a touch of weakness in his mouth, but this was shaded and half hidden by a full mustache that made much forgivable to beauty-loving eyes.

It was generally conceded that Mrs. Oakley was a hostess whose guests had no awkward half-hour before dinner. No praise could be higher than this, and tonight she had no need to exert herself to maintain this reputation. Her brother-in-law was the life of the assembly; he had wit and daring, and about him there was just that hint of charming danger that made him irresistible to women. The guests heard the dinner announced with surprise,—an unusual thing, except in this house.

Both Maurice Oakley and his wife looked fondly at the artist as he went in with Claire Lessing. He was talking animatedly to the girl, having changed the general trend of the conversation to a manner and tone directed more particularly to her. While she listened to him, her face glowed and her eyes shone with a light that every man could not bring into them.

As Maurice and his wife followed him with their gaze, the same thought was in their minds, and it had not just come to them. Why could not Francis marry Claire Lessing and settle in America, instead of going back ever and again to that life in the Latin Quarter? They did not believe that it was a bad life or a dissipated one, but from the little that they had seen of it when they were in Paris, it was at least a bit too free and unconventional for their traditions. There were, too, temptations which must assail any man of Francis's looks and talents. They had perfect faith in the strength of his manhood, of course; but could they have had their way, it would have been their will to hedge him about so that no breath of evil invitation could have come nigh to him.

But this younger brother, this half ward of theirs, was an unruly member. He talked and laughed, rode and walked, with Claire Lessing with the same free abandon, the same show of uninterested good comradeship, that he had used towards her when they were boy and girl together. There was not a shade more of warmth or self-consciousness in his manner towards her than there had been fifteen years before. In fact, there was less, for there had been a time, when he was six and Claire three, that Francis, with a boldness that the lover of maturer years tries vainly to attain, had announced to Claire that he was going to marry her. But he had never renewed this declaration when it came time that it would carry weight with it.

They made a fine picture as they sat together tonight. One seeing them could hardly help thinking on the instant that they were made for each other. Something in the woman's face, in her expression perhaps, supplied a palpable lack in the man. The strength of her mouth and chin helped the weakness of his. She was the sort of woman who, if ever he came to a great moral crisis in his life, would be able to save him if she were near. And yet he was going away from her, giving up the pearl that he had only to put out his hand to take.

Some of these thoughts were in the minds of the brother and sister now.

"Five years does seem a long while," Francis was saying, "but if a man accomplishes anything, after all, it seems only a short time to look back upon."

"All time is short to look back upon. It is the looking forward to it that counts. It doesn't, though, with a man, I suppose. He's doing something all the while."

"Yes, a man is always doing something, even if only waiting, but waiting is such unheroic business."

"That is the part that usually falls to a woman's lot. I have no doubt that some dark-eyed mademoiselle is waiting for you now."

Francis laughed and flushed hotly. Claire noted the flush and wondered at it. Had she indeed hit upon the real point? Was that the reason that he was so anxious to get back to Paris? The thought struck a chill through her gaiety. She did not want to be suspicious, but what was the cause of that tell-tale flush? He was not a man easily disconcerted; then why so to-night? But her companion talked on with such innocent composure that she believed herself mistaken as to the reason for his momentary confusion.

Someone cried gayly across the table to her: "Oh, Miss Claire, you will not dare to talk with such little awe to our friend when he comes back with his ribbons and his medals. Why, we shall all have to bow to you, Frank!"

"You're wronging me, Esterton," said Francis. "No foreign decoration could ever be to me as much as the flower of approval from the fair women of my own State."

"Hear!" cried the ladies.

"Trust artists and poets to pay pretty compliments, and this wily friend of mine pays his at my expense."

"A good bit of generalship, that, Frank," an old military man broke in. "Esterton opened the breach and you at once galloped in. That's the highest art of war."

Claire was looking at her companion. Had he meant the approval of the women, or was it one woman that he cared for? Had the speech had a hidden meaning for her? She could never tell. She could not understand this man, who had been so much to her for so long, and yet did not seem to know it; who was full of romance and fire and passion, and yet looked at her beauty with the eyes of a mere comrade. She sighed as she rose with the rest of the women to leave the table.

The men lingered over their cigars. The wine was old and the stories new. What more could they ask? There was a strong glow in Francis Oakley's face, and his laugh was frequent and ringing. Some discussion came up which sent him running up to his room for a bit of evidence. When he came down it was not to come directly to the dining-room. He paused in the hall and dispatched a servant to bring his brother to him.

Maurice found him standing weakly against the railing of the stairs. Something in his air impressed his brother strangely.

"What is it, Francis?" he questioned, hurrying to him.

"I have just discovered a considerable loss," was the reply in a grieved voice.

"If it is no worse than loss, I am glad; but what is it?"

"Every cent of money that I had to secure my letter of credit is gone from my bureau."

"What? When did it disappear?"

"I went to my bureau to-night for something and found the money gone; then I remembered that when I opened it two days ago I must have left the key in the lock, as I found it to-night."

"It's a bad business, but don't let's talk of it now. Come, let's go back to our guests. Don't look so cut up about it, Frank, old man. It isn't as bad as it might be, and you mustn't show a gloomy face to-night."

The younger man pulled himself together, and reentered the room with his brother. In a few minutes his gaiety had apparently returned.

When they rejoined the ladies, even their quick eyes could detect in his demeanour no trace of the annoying thing that had occurred. His face did not change until, with a wealth of fervent congratulations, he had bade the last guest good-bye.

Then he turned to his brother. "When Leslie is in bed, come into the library. I will wait for you there," he said, and walked sadly away.

"Poor, foolish Frank," mused his brother, "as if the loss could matter to him."

CHAPTER 3

The Theft

FRANK WAS VERY PALE when his brother finally came to him at the appointed place. He sat limply in his chair, his eyes fixed upon the floor.

"Come, brace up now, Frank, and tell me about it."

At the sound of his brother's voice he started and looked up as though he had been dreaming.

"I don't know what you'll think of me, Maurice," he said; "I have never before been guilty of such criminal carelessness."

"Don't stop to accuse yourself. Our only hope in this matter lies in prompt action. Where was the money?"

"In the oak cabinet and lying in the bureau drawer. Such a thing as a theft seemed so foreign to this place that I was never very particular about the box. But I did not know until I went to it to-night that the last time I had opened it I had forgotten to take the key out. It all flashed over me in a second when I saw it shining there. Even then I didn't suspect anything. You don't know how I felt to open that cabinet and find all my money gone. It's awful."

"Don't worry. How much was there in all?"

"Nine hundred and eighty-six dollars, most of which, I am ashamed to say, I had accepted from you."

"You have no right to talk that way, Frank; you know I do not begrudge a cent you want. I have never felt that my father did quite right in leaving me the bulk of the fortune; but we won't discuss that now. What I want you to understand, though, is that the money is yours as well as mine, and you are always welcome to it."

The artist shook his head. "No, Maurice," he said, "I can accept no more from you. I have already used up all my own money and too much of yours in this hopeless fight. I don't suppose I was ever cut out for an artist, or I'd have done something really notable in this time, and would not be a burden upon those who care for me. No, I'll give up going to Paris and find some work to do."

"Frank, Frank, be silent. This is nonsense. Give up your art? You shall not do it. You shall go to Paris as usual. Leslie and I have perfect faith in you. You shall not give up on account of this misfortune. What are the few paltry dollars to me or to you?"

"Nothing, nothing, I know. It isn't the money. It's the principle of the thing."

"Principle be hanged! You go back to Paris to-morrow, just as you had planned. I do not ask it. I command it."

The younger man looked up quickly.

"Pardon me, Frank, for using those words and at such a time. You know how near my heart your success lies, and to hear you talk of giving it all up makes me forget myself. Forgive me, but you'll go back, won't you?"

"You are too good, Maurice," said Frank impulsively, "and I will go back, and I'll try to redeem myself."

"There is no redeeming of yourself to do, my dear

boy; all you have to do is to mature yourself. We'll have a detective down and see what we can do in this matter."

Frank gave a scarcely perceptible start. "I do so hate such things," he said; "and, anyway, what's the use? They'll never find out where the stuff went to."

"Oh, you need not be troubled in this matter. I know that such things must jar on your delicate nature. But I am a plain hard-headed business man, and I can attend to it without distaste."

"But I hate to shove everything unpleasant off on you. It's what I've been doing all my life."

"Never mind that. Now tell me, who was the last person you remember in your room?"

"Oh, Esterton was up there awhile before dinner. But he was not alone two minutes."

"Why, he would be out of the question anyway. Who else?"

"Hamilton was up yesterday."

"Yes, for a while. His boy, Joe, shaved me, and Jack was up for a while brushing my clothes."

"Then it lies between Jack and Joe?"

Frank hesitated.

"Neither one was left alone, though."

"Then only Hamilton and Esterton have been alone for any time in your room since you left the key in your cabinet?"

"Those are the only ones of whom I know anything. What others went in during the day, of course, I know nothing about. It couldn't have been either Esterton or Hamilton."

"Not Esterton, no."

"And Hamilton is beyond suspicion."

"No servant is beyond suspicion."

"I would trust Hamilton anywhere," said Frank stoutly, "and with anything."

"That's noble of you, Frank, and I would have done the same, but we must remember that we are not in the old days now. The negroes are becoming less faithful and less contented, and more's the pity, and a deal more ambitious, although I have never had any unfaithfulness on the part of Hamilton to complain of before."

"Then do not condemn him now."

"I shall not condemn any one until I have proof positive of his guilt or such clear circumstantial evidence that my reason is satisfied."

"I do not believe that you will ever have that against old Hamilton."

"This spirit of trust does you credit, Frank, and I very much hope that you may be right. But as soon as a negro like Hamilton learns the value of money and begins to earn it, at the same time he begins to covet some easy and rapid way of securing it. The old negro knew nothing of the value of money. When he stole, he stole hams and bacon and chickens. These were his immediate necessities and the things he valued. The present laughs at this tendency without knowing the cause. The present negro resents the laugh, and he has learned to value other things than those which satisfy his belly."

Frank looked bored.

"But pardon me for boring you. I know you want to go to bed. Go ahead and leave everything to me."

The young man reluctantly withdrew, and Maurice went to the telephone and rung up the police station.

As Maurice had said, he was a plain, hard-headed business man, and it took very few words for him to put the Chief of Police in possession of the principal facts of the case. A detective was detailed to take charge of the case, and was started immediately, so that he might be upon the ground as soon after the commission of the crime as possible.

When he came he insisted that if he was to do anything he must question the robbed man and search his room at once. Oakley protested, but the detective was adamant. Even now the presence in the room of a man uninitiated into the mysteries of criminal methods might be destroying the last vestige of a really important clue. The master of the house had no alternative save to yield. Together they went to the artist's room. A light shone out through the crack under the door.

"I am sorry to disturb you again, Frank, but may we come in?"

"Who is with you?"

"The detective."

"I did not know he was to come to-night."

"The chief thought it better."

"All right in a moment."

There was a sound of moving around, and in a short time the young fellow, partly undressed, opened the door.

To the detective's questions he answered in substance what he had told before. He also brought out the cabinet. It was a strong oak box, uncarven, but bound at the edges with brass. The key was still in the lock, where Frank had left it on discovering his loss. They raised the lid. The cabinet contained two compartments, one for letters and a smaller one for jewels and trinkets.

"When you opened this cabinet, your money was gone?"

"Yes."

"Were any of your papers touched?"

"No."

"How about your jewels?"

"I have but few and they were elsewhere."

The detective examined the room carefully, its approaches, and the hall-ways without. He paused knowingly at a window that overlooked the flat top of a porch.

"Do you ever leave this window open?"

"It is almost always so."

"Is this porch on the front of the house?"

"No, on the side."

"What else is out that way?"

Frank and Maurice looked at each other. The younger man hesitated and put his hand to his head. Maurice answered grimly, "My butler's cottage is on that side and a little way back."

"Uh huh! and your butler is, I believe, the Hamilton whom the young gentleman mentioned some time ago."

"Yes."

Frank's face was really very white now. The detective nodded again.

"I think I have a clue," he said simply. "I will be here again to-morrow morning."

"But I shall be gone," said Frank.

"You will hardly be needed, anyway."

The artist gave a sigh of relief. He hated to be involved in unpleasant things. He went as far as the outer door with his brother and the detective. As he bade the officer good-night and hurried up the hall, Frank put his hand to his head again with a convulsive gesture, as if struck by a sudden pain.

"Come, come, Frank, you must take a drink now and go to bed," said Oakley.

"I am completely unnerved."

"I know it, and I am no less shocked than you. But we've got to face it like men."

They passed into the dining room, where Maurice

poured out some brandy for his brother and himself. "Who would have thought it?" he asked, as he tossed his own down.

"Not I. I had hoped against hope up until the last that it would turn out to be a mistake."

"Nothing angers me so much as being deceived by the man I have helped and trusted. I should feel the sting of all this much less if the thief had come from the outside, broken in, and robbed me, but this, after all these years, is too low."

"Don't be hard on a man, Maurice; one never knows what prompts him to do a deed. And this evidence is all circumstantial."

"It is plain enough for me. You are entirely too kind-hearted, Frank. But I see that this thing has worn you out. You must not stand here talking. Go to bed, for you must be fresh for to-morrow morning's journey to New York."

Frank Oakley turned away towards his room. His face was haggard, and he staggered as he walked. His brother looked after him with a pitying and affectionate gaze.

"Poor fellow," he said, "he is so delicately constructed that he cannot stand such shocks as these"; and then he added: "To think of that black hound's treachery! I'll give him all that the law sets down for him."

He found Mrs. Oakley asleep when he reached the room, but he awakened her to tell her the story. She was horror-struck. It was hard to have to believe this awful thing of an old servant, but she agreed with him that Hamilton must be made an example of when the time came. Before that, however, he must not know that he was suspected.

They fell asleep, he with thoughts of anger and revenge, and she grieved and disappointed.

CHAPTER 4

From a Clear Sky

THE INMATES OF THE Oakley house had not been long in their beds before Hamilton was out of his and rousing his own little household.

"You, Joe," he called to his son, "git up f'om daih an' come right hyeah. You got to he'p me befo' you go to any shop dis mo'nin'. You, Kitty, stir yo' stumps, miss. I know yo' ma's a-dressin' now. Ef she ain't, I bet I'll be aftah huh in a minute, too. You all layin' 'roun', snoozin' w'en you all des' pint'ly know dis is de mo'nin' Mistah Frank go 'way f'om hyeah."

It was a cool Autumn morning, fresh and dew-washed. The sun was just rising, and a cool clear breeze was blowing across the land. The blue smoke from the "house," where the fire was already going, whirled fantastically over the roofs like a belated ghost. It was just the morning to doze in comfort, and so thought all of Berry's household except himself. Loud was the complaining as they threw themselves out of bed. They maintained that it was an altogether unearthly hour to get up. Even Mrs. Hamilton added her protest, until she suddenly remembered what morning it was, when she hurried into her clothes and set about getting the family's breakfast.

The good-humour of all of them returned when they were seated about their table with some of the good things of the night before set out, and the talk ran cheerily around.

"I do declaih," said Hamilton, "you all's as bad as dem white people was las' night. De way dey waded into dat food was a caution." He chuckled with delight at the recollection.

"I reckon dat's what dey come fu'. I wasn't payin' so much 'tention to what dey eat as to de way dem women was dressed. Why, Mis' Jedge Hill was des' mo'n go'geous."

"Oh, yes, ma, an' Miss Lessing wasn't no ways behin' her," put in Kitty.

Joe did not condescend to join in the conversation, but contented himself with devouring the good things and aping the manners of the young men whom he knew had been among last night's guests.

"Well, I got to be goin'," said Berry, rising. "There'll be early breakfas' at de 'house' dis mo'nin', so's Mistah Frank kin ketch de fus' train."

He went out cheerily to his work. No shadow of impending disaster depressed his spirits. No cloud obscured his sky. He was a simple, easy man, and he saw nothing in the manner of the people whom he served that morning at breakfast, save a natural grief at parting from each other. He did not even take the trouble to inquire who the strange white man was who hung about the place.

When it came time for the young man to leave, with the privilege of an old servitor Berry went up to him to bid him good-bye. He held out his hand to him, and with a glance at his brother, Frank took it and shook it cordially. "Good-bye, Berry," he said. Maurice could hardly restrain his anger at the sight, but his wife was moved to tears at her brother-in-law's generosity.

The last sight they saw as the carriage rolled away towards the station was Berry standing upon the steps waving a hearty farewell and god-speed.

"How could you do it, Frank?" gasped his brother, as soon as they had driven well out of hearing.

"Hush, Maurice," said Mrs. Oakley gently; "I think it was very noble of him."

"Oh, I felt sorry for the poor fellow," was Frank's reply. "Promise me you won't be too hard on him, Maurice. Give him a little scare and let him go. He's possibly buried the money, anyhow."

"I shall deal with him as he deserves."

The young man sighed and was silent the rest of the way.

"Whether I fail or succeed, you will always think well of me, Maurice?" he said in parting; "and if I don't come up to your expectations, well—forgive me—that's all."

His brother wrung his hand. "You will always come up to my expectations, Frank," he said. "Won't he, Leslie?"

"He will always be our Frank, our good, generous-hearted, noble boy. God bless him!"

The young fellow bade them a hearty good-bye, and they, knowing what his feelings must be, spared him the prolonging of the strain. They waited in the carriage, and he waved to them as the train rolled out of the station.

"He seems to be sad at going," said Mrs. Oakley.

"Poor fellow, the affair of last night has broken him up considerably, but I'll make Berry pay for every pang of anxiety that my brother has suffered."

"Don't be revengeful, Maurice; you know what brother Frank asked of you."

"He is gone and will never know what happens, so I may be as revengeful as I wish."

The detective was waiting on the lawn when Maurice Oakley returned. They went immediately to the library, Oakley walking with the firm, hard tread of a man who is both exasperated and determined, and the officer gliding along with the cat-like step which is one of the attributes of his profession.

"Well?" was the impatient man's question as soon as the door closed upon him.

"I have some more information that may or may not be of importance."

"Out with it; maybe I can tell."

"First, let me ask you if you had any reason to believe that your butler had any resources of his own, say to the amount of three or four hundred dollars?"

"Certainly not. I pay him thirty dollars a month, and his wife fifteen dollars, and with keeping up his lodges and the way he dresses that girl, he can't save very much."

"You know that he has money in the bank?"

"No."

"Well, he has. Over eight hundred dollars."

"What? Berry? It must be the pickings of years."

"And yesterday it was increased by five hundred more."

"The scoundrel!"

"How was your brother's money, in bills?"

"It was in large bills and gold, with some silver."

"Berry's money was almost all in bills of a small denomination and silver."

"A poor trick; it could easily have been changed."

"Not such a sum without exciting comment."

"He may have gone to several places."

"But he had only a day to do it in."

"Then someone must have been his accomplice."

"That remains to be proven."

"Nothing remains to be proven. Why, it's as clear as day that the money he has is the result of a long series of peculations, and that this last is the result of his first large theft."

"That must be made clear to the law."

"It shall be."

"I should advise, though, no open proceedings against this servant until further evidence to establish his guilt is found."

"If the evidence satisfies me, it must be sufficient to satisfy any ordinary jury. I demand his immediate arrest."

"As you will, sir. Will you have him called here and question him, or will you let me question him at once?"

"Yes."

Oakley struck the bell, and Berry himself answered it.

"You're just the man we want," said Oakley, shortly.

Berry looked astonished.

"Shall I question him," asked the officer, "or will you?"

"I will. Berry, you deposited five hundred dollars at the bank yesterday?"

"Well, suh, Mistah Oakley," was the grinning reply, "ef you ain't de beatenes' man to fin' out things I evah seen."

The employer half rose from his chair. His face was livid with anger. But at a sign from the detective he strove to calm himself.

"You had better let me talk to Berry, Mr. Oakley," said the officer.

Oakley nodded. Berry was looking distressed and excited. He seemed not to understand it at all.

"Berry," the officer pursued, "you admit having deposited five hundred dollars in the bank yesterday?"

"Sut'ny. Dey ain't no reason why I shouldn't admit it, 'ceptin' erroun' ermong dese jealous niggahs."

"Uh huh! well, now, where did you get this money?"

"Why, I wo'ked fu' it, o' co'se, whaih you s'pose I got it? 'Tain't drappin' off trees, I reckon, not roun' dis pa't of de country."

"You worked for it? You must have done a pretty big job to have got so much money all in a lump?"

"But I didn't git it in a lump. Why, man, I've been savin' dat money fu' mo'n fo' yeahs."

"More than four years? Why didn't you put it in the bank as you got it?"

"Why, mos'ly it was too small, an' so I des' kep' it in a ol' sock. I tol' Fannie dat some day ef de bank didn't bus' wid all de res' I had, I'd put it in too. She was alus sayin' it was too much to have layin' 'roun' de house. But I des' tol' huh dat no robber wasn't goin' to bothah de po' niggah down in de ya'd wid de rich white man up at de house. But fin'lly I listened to huh an' sposited it yistiddy."

"You're a liar! you're a liar, you black thief!" Oakley broke in impetuously. "You have learned your lesson well, but you can't cheat me. I know where that money came from."

"Calm yourself, Mr. Oakley, calm yourself."

"I will not calm myself. Take him away. He shall not stand here and lie to me."

Berry had suddenly turned ashen.

"You say you know whaih dat money come f'om? Whaih?"

"You stole it, you thief, from my brother Frank's room."

"Stole it! My Gawd, Mistah Oakley, you believed a thing lak dat aftah all de yeahs I been wid you?"

"You've been stealing all along."

"Why, what shell I do?" said the servant helplessly. "I tell you, Mistah Oakley, ask Fannie. She'll know how long I been a-savin' dis money."

"I'll ask no one."

"I think it would be better to call his wife, Oakley."

"Well, call her, but let this matter be done with soon."

Fannie was summoned, and when the matter was explained to her, first gave evidences of giving way to grief, but when the detective began to question her, she calmed herself and answered directly just as her husband had.

"Well posted," sneered Oakley. "Arrest that man."

Berry had begun to look more hopeful during Fannie's recital, but now the ashen look came back into his face. At the word "arrest" his wife collapsed utterly, and sobbed on her husband's shoulder.

"Send the woman away."

"I won't go," cried Fannie stoutly; "I'll stay right hyeah by my husband. You sha'n't drive me away f'om him."

Berry turned to his employer. "You b'lieve dat I stole f'om dis house aftah all de yeahs I've been in it, aftah de caih I took of yo' money an' yo' valybles, aftah de way I've put you to bed f'om many a dinnah, an' you woke up to fin' all yo' money safe? Now, can you b'lieve dis?"

His voice broke, and he ended with a cry.

"Yes, I believe it, you thief, yes. Take him away."

Berry's eyes were bloodshot as he replied, "Den, damn you! damn you! ef dat's all dese yeahs counted fu', I wish I had a-stoled it."

Oakley made a step forward, and his man did likewise, but the officer stepped between them.

"Take that damned hound away, or, by God! I'll do him violence!"

The two men stood fiercely facing each other; then the handcuffs were snapped on the servant's wrist.

"No, no," shrieked Fannie, "you mustn't, you mustn't. Oh, my Gawd! he ain't no thief. I'll go to Mis' Oakley. She nevah will believe it." She sped from the room.

The commotion had called a crowd of curious servants into the hall. Fannie hardly saw them as she dashed among them, crying for her mistress. In a moment she returned, dragging Mrs. Oakley by the hand.

"Tell 'em, oh, tell 'em, Miss Leslie, dat you don't believe it. Don't let 'em 'rest Berry."

"Why, Fannie, I can't do anything. It all seems perfectly plain, and Mr. Oakley knows better than any of us, you know."

Fannie, her last hope gone, flung herself on the floor, crying, "O Gawd! O Gawd! he's gone fu' sho'!"

Her husband bent over her, the tears dropping from his eyes. "Nevah min', Fannie," he said, "nevah min'. Hit's boun' to come out all right."

She raised her head, and seizing his manacled hands pressed them to her breast, wailing in a low monotone, "Gone! gone!"

They disengaged her hands, and led Berry away.

"Take her out," said Oakley sternly to the servants; and they lifted her up and carried her away in a sort of dumb stupor that was half a swoon.

They took her to her little cottage, and laid her down until she could come to herself and the full horror of her situation burst upon her.

CHAPTER 5

The Justice of Men

THE ARREST OF Berry Hamilton on the charge preferred by his employer was the cause of unusual commotion in the town. Both the accuser and the accused were well known to the citizens, white and black,—Maurice Oakley as a solid man of business, and Berry as an honest, sensible negro, and the pink of good servants. The evening papers had a full story of the crime, which closed by saying that the prisoner had amassed a considerable sum of money, it was very likely from a long series of smaller peculations.

It seems a strange irony upon the force of right living, that this man, who had never been arrested before, who had never even been suspected of wrong-doing, should find so few who even at the first telling doubted the story of his guilt. Many people began to remember things that had looked particularly suspicious in his dealings. Some others said, "I didn't think it of him." There were only a few who dared to say, "I don't believe it of him."

The first act of his lodge, "The Tribe of Benjamin," whose treasurer he was, was to have his accounts audited, when they should have been visiting him with comfort, and they seemed personally grieved when his books were found to be straight. The A. M. E. church, of which he had been an honest and active member, hastened to disavow sympathy with him, and to purge itself of contamination by turning him out. His friends were afraid to visit him and were silent when his enemies gloated. On every side one might have asked, Where is charity? and gone away empty.

In the black people of the town the strong influence of slavery was still operative, and with one accord they turned away from one of their own kind upon whom had been set the ban of the white people's displeasure. If they had sympathy, they dared not show it. Their own interests, the safety of their own positions and firesides, demanded that they stand aloof from the criminal. Not then, not now, nor has it ever been true, although it has been claimed, that negroes either harbor or sympathise with the criminal of their kind. They did not dare to do it before the sixties. They do not dare to do it now. They have brought down as a heritage from the days of their bondage both fear and disloyalty. So Berry was unbefriended while the storm raged around him. The cell where they had placed him was kind to him, and he could not hear the envious and sneering comments that went on about him. This was kind, for the tongues of his enemies were not.

"Tell me, tell me," said one, "you needn't tell me dat a bird kin fly so high dat he don' have to come down some time. An' w'en he do light, honey, my Lawd, how he flop!"

"Mistah Rich Niggah," said another. "He wanted to dress his wife an' chillen lak white folks, did he? Well, he foun' out, he foun' out. By de time de jedge git thoo wid him he won't be hol'in' his haid so high."

"W'y, dat gal o' his'n," broke in old Isaac Brown

indignantly, "w'y, she wouldn' speak to my gal, Minty, when she met huh on de street. I reckon she come down off'n huh high hoss now."

The fact of the matter was that Minty Brown was no better than she should have been, and did not deserve to be spoken to. But none of this was taken into account either by the speaker or the hearers. The man was down, it was time to strike.

The women too joined their shrill voices to the general cry, and were loud in their abuse of the Hamiltons and in disparagement of their high-toned airs.

"I knowed it, I knowed it," mumbled one old crone, rolling her bleared and jealous eyes with glee. "W'enevah you see niggahs gittin' so high dat dey own folks ain' good enough fu' 'em, look out."

"W'y, la, Aunt Chloe, I knowed it too. Dem people got so owdacious proud dat dey wouldn't walk up to de collection table no mo' at chu'ch, but allus set an' waited twell de basket was passed erroun'."

"Hit's de livin' trufe, an' I's been seein' it all 'long. I ain't said nuffin', but I knowed what 'uz gwine to happen. Ol' Chloe ain't lived all dese yeahs fu' nuffin', an' ef she got de gif' o' secon' sight, 'tain't fu' huh to say."

The women suddenly became interested in this half assertion, and the old hag, seeing that she had made the desired impression, lapsed into silence.

The whites were not neglecting to review and comment on the case also. It had been long since so great a bit of wrong-doing in a negro had given them cause for speculation and recrimination.

"I tell you," said old Horace Talbot, who was noted for his kindliness towards people of colour. "I tell you, I pity that darky more than I blame him. Now, here's my theory." They were in the bar of the Continental Hotel, and the old gentleman sipped his liquor as he talked. "It's just like this: The North thought they were doing a great thing when they come down here and freed all the slaves. They thought they were doing a great thing, and I'm not saying a word against them. I give them the credit for having the courage of their convictions. But I maintain that they were all wrong, now, in turning these people loose upon the country the way they did, without knowledge of what the first principle of liberty was. The natural result is that these people are irresponsible. They are unacquainted with the ways of our higher civilisation, and it'll take them a long time to learn. You know Rome wasn't built in a day. I know Berry and I've known him for a long while, and a politer, likelier darky than him you would have to go far to find. And I haven't the least doubt in the world that he took that money absolutely without a thought of wrong, sir, absolutely. He saw it. He took it, and to his mental process, that was the end of it. To him there was no injury inflicted on any one; there was no crime committed. His elemental reasoning was simply this: This man has more money than I have; here is some of his surplus,—I'll just take it. Why, gentlemen, I maintain that that man took that money with the same innocence of purpose with which one of our servants a few years ago would have appropriated a stray ham."

"I disagree with you entirely, Mr. Talbot," broke in Mr. Beachfield Davis, who was a mighty hunter.— "Make mine the same, Jerry, only add a little syrup.—I disagree with you. It's simply total depravity, that's all. All niggers are alike, and there's no use trying to do anything with them. Look at that man, Dodson, of mine. I had one of the finest young hounds in the State. You know that white pup of mine, Mr. Talbot, that I bought from Hiram Gaskins? Mighty fine breed. Well, I was spendin' all my time and patience trainin' that dog in the daytime. At night I put him in that nigger's care to feed and bed. Well, do you know, I came home the other night and found that black rascal gone? I went out to see if the dog was properly bedded, and by Jove, the dog was gone too. Then I got suspicious. When a nigger and a dog go out together at night, one draws certain conclusions. I thought I had heard bayin' way out towards the edge of the town. So I stayed outside and watched. In about an hour here came Dodson with a possum hung over his shoulder and my dog trottin' at his heels. He'd been possum huntin' with my hound—with the finest hound in the State, sir. Now, I appeal to you all, gentlemen, if that ain't total depravity, what is total depravity?"

"Not total depravity, Beachfield, I maintain, but the very irresponsibility of which I have spoken. Why, gentlemen, I foresee the day when these people themselves shall come to us Southerners of their own accord and ask to be re-enslaved until such time as they shall be fit for freedom." Old Horace was nothing if not logical.

"Well, do you think there's any doubt of the darky's guilt?" asked Colonel Saunders hesitatingly. He was the only man who had ever thought of such a possibility. They turned on him as if he had been some strange, unnatural animal.

"Any doubt!" cried Old Horace.

"Any doubt!" exclaimed Mr. Davis.

"Any doubt" almost shrieked the rest. "Why, there can be no doubt. Why, Colonel, what are you thinking of? Tell us who has got the money if he hasn't? Tell us where on earth the nigger got the money he's been putting in the bank? Doubt? Why, there isn't the least doubt about it."

"Certainly, certainly," said the Colonel, "but I thought, of course, he might have saved it. There are several of those people, you know, who do a little business and have bank accounts."

"Yes, but they are in some sort of business. This man makes only thirty dollars a month. Don't you see?"

The Colonel saw, or said he did. And he did not answer what he might have answered, that Berry had no rent and no board to pay. His clothes came from his master, and Kitty and Fannie looked to their mistress for the larger number of their supplies. He did not call to their minds that Fannie herself made fifteen dollars a month, and that for two years Joe had been supporting himself. These things did not come up, and as far as the opinion of the gentlemen assembled in the Continental bar went, Berry was already proven guilty.

As for the prisoner himself, after the first day when he had pleaded "Not guilty" and been bound over to the Grand Jury, he had fallen into a sort of dazed calm that was like the stupor produced by a drug. He took little heed of what went on around him. The shock had been too sudden for him, and it was as if his reason had been for the time unseated. That it was not permanently overthrown was evidenced by his waking to the most acute pain and grief whenever Fannie came to him. Then he would toss and moan and give vent to his sorrow in passionate complaints.

"I didn't tech his money, Fannie—you know I didn't. I wo'ked fu' every cent of dat money, an' I saved it myself. Oh, I'll nevah be able to git a job ag'in. Me in de lock-up—me, aftah all dese yeahs!"

Beyond this, apparently, his mind could not go. That his detention was anything more than temporary never seemed to enter his mind. That he would be convicted and sentenced was as far from possibility as the skies from the earth. If he saw visions of a long sojourn in prison, it was only as a nightmare half consciously experienced and which with the struggle must give way before the waking.

Fannie was utterly hopeless. She had laid down whatever pride had been hers and gone to plead with Maurice Oakley for her husband's freedom, and she had seen his hard, set face. She had gone upon her knees before his wife to cite Berry's long fidelity.

"Oh, Mis' Oakley," she cried, "ef he did steal de money, we've got enough saved to mek it good. Let him go! let him go!"

"Then you admit that he did steal?" Mrs. Oakley had taken her up sharply.

"Oh, I didn't say dat; I didn't mean dat."

"That will do, Fannie. I understand perfectly. You should have confessed that long ago."

"But I ain't confessin'! I ain't! He didn't——"

"You may go."

The stricken woman reeled out of her mistress's presence, and Mrs. Oakley told her husband that night, with tears in her eyes, how disappointed she was with Fannie,—that the woman had known it all along, and had only just confessed. It was just one more link in the chain that was surely and not too slowly forging itself about Berry Hamilton.

Of all the family Joe was the only one who burned with a fierce indignation. He knew that his father was innocent, and his very helplessness made a fever in his soul. Dandy as he was, he was loyal, and when he saw his mother's tears and his sister's shame, something rose within him that had it been given play might have made a man of him, but, being crushed, died and rotted, and in the compost it made, all the evil of his nature flourished. The looks and gibes of his fellow-employees at the barber-shop forced him to leave his work there. Kit, bowed with shame and grief, dared not appear upon the streets, where the girls who had envied her now hooted at her. So the little family was shut in upon itself away from fellowship and sympathy.

Joe went seldom to see his father. He was not heartless; but the citadel of his long-desired and much vaunted manhood trembled before the sight of his father's abject misery. The lines came round his lips, and lines too must have come round his heart. Poor fellow, he was too young for this forcing process, and in the hothouse of pain he only grew an acrid, unripe cynic.

At the sitting of the Grand Jury Berry was indicted. His trial followed soon, and the town turned out to see it. Some came to laugh and scoff, but these, his enemies, were silenced by the spectacle of his grief. In vain the lawyer whom he had secured showed that the evidence against him proved nothing. In vain he produced proof of the slow accumulation of what the man had. In vain he pleaded the man's former good name. The judge and the jury saw otherwise. Berry was convicted. He was given ten years at hard labour.

He hardly looked as if he could live out one as he heard his sentence. But Nature was kind and relieved him of the strain. With a cry as if his heart were bursting, he started up and fell forward on his face unconscious. Some one, a bit more brutal than the rest, said, "It's five dollars' fine every time a nigger faints," but no one laughed. There was something too portentous, too tragic in the degradation of this man.

Maurice Oakley sat in the court-room, grim and relentless. As soon as the trial was over, he sent for Fannie, who still kept the cottage in the yard.

"You must go," he said. "You can't stay here any longer. I want none of your breed about me."

And Fannie bowed her head and went away from him in silence.

All the night long the women of the Hamilton household lay in bed and wept, clinging to each other in their grief. But Joe did not go to sleep. Against all their entreaties, he stayed up. He put out the light and sat staring into the gloom with hard, burning eyes.

CHAPTER 6

Outcasts

WHAT PARTICULARLY IRRITATED Maurice Oakley was that Berry should to the very last keep up his claim of innocence. He reiterated it to the very moment that the train which was bearing him away pulled out of the station. There had seldom been seen such an example of criminal hardihood, and Oakley was hardened thereby to greater severity in dealing with the convict's wife. He began to urge her more strongly to move, and she, dispirited and humiliated by what had come to her, looked vainly about her for the way to satisfy his demands. With her natural protector gone, she felt more weak and helpless than she had thought it possible to feel. It was hard enough to face the world. But to have to ask something of it was almost more than she could bear.

With the conviction of her husband the last five hundred dollars had been confiscated as belonging to the stolen money, but their former deposit remained untouched. With this she had the means at her disposal to tide over their present days of misfortune. It was not money she lacked, but confidence. Some inkling of the world's attitude towards her, guiltless though she was, reached her and made her afraid.

Her desperation, however, would not let her give way to fear, so she set forth to look for another house. Joe and Kit saw her go as if she were starting on an expedition into a strange country. In all their lives they had known no home, save the little cottage in Oakley's yard. Here they had toddled as babies and played as children and been happy and carefree. There had been times when they had complained and wanted a home off by themselves, like others whom they knew. They had not failed, either, to draw unpleasant comparisons between their mode of life and the old plantation quarters system. But now all this was forgotten, and there were only grief and anxiety that they must leave the place and in such a way.

Fannie went out with little hope in her heart, and a short while after she was gone Joe decided to follow her and make an attempt to get work.

"I'll go an' see what I kin do, anyway, Kit. 'Tain't much use, I reckon, trying to get into a bahbah shop where they shave white folks, because all the white folks are down on us. I'll try one of the coloured shops."

This was something of a condescension for Berry Hamilton's son. He had never yet shaved a black chin or put shears to what he termed "naps," and he was proud of it. He thought, though, that after the training he had received from the superior "Tonsorial Parlours" where he had been employed, he had but to ask for a place and he would be gladly accepted.

It is strange how all the foolish little vaunting things that a man says in days of prosperity wax a giant crop around him in the days of his adversity. Berry Hamilton's son found this out almost as soon as he had applied at the first of the coloured shops for work.

"Oh, no, suh," said the proprietor, "I don't think we

got anything fu' you to do; you're a white man's bahbah. We don't shave nothin' but niggahs hyeah, an' we shave 'em in de light o' day an' on de groun' flo'."

"W'y, I hyeah you say dat you couldn't git a paih of sheahs thoo a niggah's naps. You ain't been practisin' lately, has you?" came from the back of the shop, where a grinning negro was scraping a fellow's face.

"Oh, yes, you're done with burr-heads, are you? But burr-heads are good enough fu' you now."

"I think," the proprietor resumed, "that I hyeahed you say you wasn't fond o' grape pickin'. Well, Josy, my son, I wouldn't begin it now, 'specially as anothah kin' o' pickin' seems to run in yo' fambly."

Joe Hamilton never knew how he got out of that shop. He only knew that he found himself upon the street outside the door, tears of anger and shame in his eyes, and the laughs and taunts of his tormentors still ringing in his ears.

It was cruel, of course it was cruel. It was brutal. But only he knew how just it had been. In his moments of pride he had said all those things, half in fun and half in earnest, and he began to wonder how he could have been so many kinds of a fool for so long without realizing it.

He had not the heart to seek another shop, for he knew that what would be known at one would be equally well known at all the rest. The hardest thing that he had to bear was the knowledge that he had shut himself out of all the chances that he now desired. He remembered with a pang the words of an old negro to whom he had once been impudent, "Nevah min', boy, nevah min'— you's bo'n, but you ain't daid!"

It was too true. He had not known then what would come. He had never dreamed that anything so terrible could overtake him. Even in his straits, however, desperation gave him a certain pluck. He would try for something else for which his own tongue had not disqualified him. With Joe, to think was to do. He went on to the Continental Hotel, where there were almost always boys wanted to "run the bells." The clerk looked him over critically. He was a bright, spruce-looking young fellow, and the man liked his looks.

"Well, I guess we can take you on," he said. "What's your name?"

"Joe," was the laconic answer. He was afraid to say more.

"Well, Joe, you go over there and sit where you see those fellows in uniform, and wait until I call the head bellman."

Young Hamilton went over and sat down on a bench which ran along the hotel corridor and where the bellman were wont to stay during the day awaiting their calls. A few of the blue-coated Mercuries were there. Upon Joe's advent they began to look askance at him and to talk among themselves. He felt his face burning as he thought of what they must be saying. Then he saw the head bellman talking to the clerk and looking in his direction. He saw him shake his head and walk away. He could have cursed him. The clerk called to him.

"I didn't know," he said,—"I didn't know that you were Berry Hamilton's boy. Now, I've got nothing against you myself. I don't hold you responsible for what your father did, but I don't believe our boys would work with you. I can't take you on."

Joe turned away to meet the grinning or contemptuous glances of the bellmen on the seat. It would have been good to be able to hurl something among them. But he was helpless.

He hastened out of the hotel, feeling that every eye was upon him, every finger pointing at him, every tongue whispering, "There goes Joe Hamilton, whose father went to the penitentiary the other day."

What should he do? He could try no more. He was prescribed, and the letters of his ban were writ large throughout the town, where all who ran might read. For a while he wandered aimlessly about and then turned dejectedly homeward. His mother had not yet come.

"Did you get a job?" was Kit's first question.

"No," he answered bitterly, "no one wants me now."

"No one wants you? Why, Joe—they—they don't think hard of us, do they?"

"I don't know what they think of ma and you, but they think hard of me, all right."

"Oh, don't you worry; it'll be all right when it blows over."

"Yes, when it all blows over; but when'll that be?"

"Oh, after a while, when we can show 'em we're all right."

Some of the girl's cheery hopefulness had come back to her in the presence of her brother's dejection, as a woman always forgets her own sorrow when some one she loves is grieving. But she could not communicate any of her feeling to Joe, who had been and seen and felt, and now sat darkly waiting his mother's return. Some presentiment seemed to tell him that, armed as she was with money to pay for what she wanted and asking for nothing without price, she would yet have no better tale to tell than he.

None of these forebodings visited the mind of Kit, and as soon as her mother appeared on the threshold she ran to her, crying, "Oh, where are we going to live, ma?"

Fannie looked at her for a moment, and then answered with a burst of tears, "Gawd knows, child, Gawd knows."

The girl stepped back astonished. "Why, why!" and then with a rush of tenderness she threw her arms about her mother's neck. "Oh, you're tired to death," she said; "that's what's the matter with you. Never mind about the house now. I've got some tea made for you, and you just take a cup."

Fannie sat down and tried to drink her tea, but she could not. It stuck in her throat, and the tears rolled down her face and fell into the shaking cup. Joe looked on silently. He had been out and he understood.

"I'll go out to-morrow and do some looking around for a house while you stay at home an' rest, ma."

Her mother looked up, the maternal instinct for the protection of her daughter at once aroused. "Oh, no, not you, Kitty," she said.

Then for the first time Joe spoke: "You'd just as well tell Kitty now, ma, for she's got to come across it anyhow."

"What you know about it? Whaih you been to?"

"I've been out huntin' work. I've been to Jones's bah-bah shop an' to the Continental Hotel." His light-brown face turned brick red with anger and shame at the memory of it. "I don't think I'll try any more."

Kitty was gazing with wide and saddening eyes at her mother.

"Were they mean to you too, ma?" she asked breathlessly.

"Mean? Oh Kitty! Kitty! you don't know what it was like. It nigh killed me. Thaih was plenty of houses an' owned by people I've knowed fu' yeahs, but not one of 'em wanted to rent to me. Some of 'em made excuses 'bout one thing er t'other, but de res' come right straight out an' said dat we'd give a neighbourhood a bad name ef we moved into it. I've almos' tramped my laigs off. I've tried every decent place I could think of, but nobody wants us."

The girl was standing with her hands clenched nervously before her. It was almost more than she could understand.

"Why, we ain't done anything," she said. "Even if they don't know any better than to believe that pa was guilty, they know we ain't done anything."

"I'd like to cut the heart out of a few of 'em," said Joe in his throat.

"It ain't goin' to do no good to look at it that a-way, Joe," his mother replied. "I know hit's ha'd, but we got to do de bes' we kin."

"What are we goin' to do?" cried the boy fiercely. "They won't let us work. They won't let us live anywhaih. Do they want us to live on the levee an' steal, like some of 'em do?"

"What are we goin' to do?" echoed Kitty helplessly. "I'd go out ef I thought I could find anythin' to work at."

"Don't you go anywhaih, child. It 'ud only be worse. De niggah men dat ust to be bowin' an' scrapin' to me an' tekin' off dey hats to me laughed in my face. I met Minty—an' she slurred me right in de street. Dey'd do worse fu' you."

In the midst of the conversation a knock came at the door. It was a messenger from the "House," as they still called Oakley's home, and he wanted them to be out of the cottage by the next afternoon, as the new servants were coming and would want the rooms.

The message was so curt, so hard and decisive, that Fannie was startled out of her grief into immediate action.

"Well, we got to go," she said, rising wearily.

"But where are we goin'?" wailed Kitty in affright. "There's no place to go to. We haven't got a house. Where'll we go?"

"Out o' town someplace as fur away from this damned hole as we kin git." The boy spoke recklessly in his anger. He had never sworn before his mother before.

She looked at him in horror. "Joe, Joe," she said, "you're mekin' it wuss. You're mekin' it ha'dah fu' me to baih when you talk dat a-way. What you mean? Whaih you think Gawd is?"

Joe remained sullenly silent. His mother's faith was too stalwart for his comprehension. There was nothing like it in his own soul to interpret it.

"We'll git de secon'-han' dealah to tek ouah things tomorrer, an' then we'll go away some place, up No'th maybe."

"Let's go to New York," said Joe.

"New Yo'k?"

They had heard of New York as a place vague and far away, a city that, like Heaven, to them had existed by faith alone. All the days of their lives they had heard of it, and it seemed to them the center of all the glory, all the wealth, and all the freedom of the world. New York. It had an alluring sound. Who would know them there? Who would look down upon them?

"It's a mighty long ways off fu' me to be sta'tin' at dis time o' life."

"We want to go a long ways off."

"I wonder what pa would think of it if he was here," put in Kitty.

"I guess he'd think we was doin' the best we could."

"Well, den, Joe," said his mother, her voice trembling with emotion at the daring step they were about to take, "you set down an' write a lettah to yo' pa, an' tell him what we goin' to do, an' to-morrer—to-morrer—we'll sta't."

Something akin to joy came into the boy's heart as he sat down to write the letter. They had taunted him, had they? They had scoffed at him. But he was going where they might never go, and some day he would come back holding his head high and pay them sneer for sneer and jibe for jibe.

The same night the commission was given to the furniture dealer who would take charge of their things and sell them when and for what he could.

From his window the next morning Maurice Oakley watched the wagon emptying the house. Then he saw Fannie come out and walk about her little garden, followed by her children. He saw her as she wiped her eyes and led the way to the side gate.

"Well, they're gone," he said to his wife. "I wonder where they're going to live."

"Oh, some of their people will take them in," replied Mrs. Oakley languidly.

Despite the fact that his mother carried with her the rest of the money drawn from the bank, Joe had suddenly stepped into the place of the man of the family. He attended to all the details of their getting away with a promptness that made it seem untrue that he had never been more than thirty miles from his native town. He was eager and excited. As the train drew out of the station, he did not look back upon the place which he hated, but Fannie and her daughter let their eyes linger upon it until the last house, the last chimney, and the last spire faded from their sight, and their tears fell and mingled as they were whirled away toward the unknown.

CHAPTER 7

In New York

To THE PROVINCIAL coming to New York for the first time, ignorant and unknown, the city presents a notable mingling of the qualities of cheeriness and gloom. If he has any eye at all for the beautiful, he cannot help experiencing a thrill as he crosses the ferry over the river filled with plying craft and catches the first sight of the spires and buildings of New York. If he have the right stuff in him, a something will take possession of him that will grip him again every time he returns to the scene and will make him long and hunger for the place when he is away from it. Later, the lights in the busy streets will bewilder and entice him. He will feel shy and helpless amid the hurrying crowds. A new emotion will take his heart as the people hasten by him,—a feeling of loneliness, almost of grief, that with all of these souls about him he knows not one and not one of them cares for him. After a while he will find a place and give a sigh of relief as he settles away from the city's sights behind his cosey blinds. It is better here, and the city is cruel and cold and unfeeling. This he will feel, perhaps, for the first half-hour, and then he will be out in it all again. He will be glad to strike elbows with the bustling mob and be happy at their indifference to him, so that he may look at them and study them. After it is all over, after he has passed through the first pangs of strangeness and homesickness, yes, even after he has got beyond the stranger's enthusiasm for the metropolis, the real fever of love for the place will begin to take hold upon him. The subtle, insidious wine of New York will begin to intoxicate him. Then, if he be wise, he will go away, any place,—yes, he will even go over to Jersey. But if he be a fool, he will stay and stay on until the town becomes all in all to him; until the very streets are his chums and certain buildings and corners his best friends. Then he is hopeless, and to live elsewhere would be death. The Bowery will be his romance, Broadway his lyric, and the Park his pastoral, the river and the glory of it all his epic, and he will look down pityingly on all the rest of humanity.

It was the afternoon of a clear October day that the Hamiltons reached New York. Fannie had some misgivings about crossing the ferry, but once on the boat these gave way to speculations as to what they should find on the other side. With the eagerness of youth to take in new impressions, Joe and Kitty were more concerned with what they saw about them than with what their future would hold, though they might well have stopped to ask some such questions. In all the great city they knew absolutely no one, and had no idea which way to go to find a stopping-place.

They looked about them for some coloured face, and finally saw one among the porters who were handling the baggage. To Joe's inquiry he gave them an address, and also proffered his advice as to the best way to reach the place. He was exceedingly polite, and he looked hard at Kitty. They found the house to which they had been directed, and were a good deal surprised at its apparent grandeur. It was a four-storied brick dwelling on Twenty-seventh Street. As they looked from the outside, they were afraid that the price of staying in such a place would be too much for their pockets. Inside, the sight of the hard, gaudily upholstered installment-plan furniture did not disillusion them, and they continued to fear that they could never stop at this fine place. But they found Mrs. Jones, the proprietress, both gracious and willing to come to terms with them.

As Mrs. Hamilton—she began to be Mrs. Hamilton now, to the exclusion of Fannie—would have described Mrs. Jones, she was a "big yellow woman." She had a broad good-natured face and a tendency to run to bust.

"Yes," she said, "I think I could arrange to take you. I could let you have two rooms, and you could use my kitchen until you decided whether you wanted to take a flat or not. I has the whole house myself, and I keeps roomers. But latah on I could fix things so's you could have the whole third floor ef you wanted to. Most o' my gent'men 's railroad gent'men, they is. I guess it must 'a' been Mr. Thomas that sent you up here."

"He was a little bright man down at de deepo."

"Yes, that's him. That's Mr. Thomas. He's always lookin' out to send someone here, because he's been here three years hisself an' he kin recommend my house."

It was a relief to the Hamiltons to find Mrs. Jones so gracious and home-like. So the matter was settled, and they took up their abode with her and sent for their baggage.

With the first pause in the rush that they had experienced since starting away from home, Mrs. Hamilton began to have time for reflection, and their condition seemed to her much better as it was. Of course, it was hard to be away from home and among strangers, but the arrangement had this advantage,—that no one knew them or could taunt them with their past trouble. She was not sure that she was going to like New York. It had a great name and was really a great place, but the very bigness of it frightened her and made her feel alone, for she knew that there could not be so many people together without a deal of wickedness. She did not argue the complement of this, that the amount of good would also be increased, but this was because to her evil was the very present factor in her life.

Joe and Kit were differently affected by what they saw about them. The boy was wild with enthusiasm and with a desire to be a part of all that the metropolis meant. In the evening he saw the young fellows passing by dressed in their spruce clothes, and he wondered with a sort of envy where they could be going. Back home there had been no place much worth going to, except church and one or two people's houses. But these young fellows seemed to show by their manners that they were neither going to church nor a family visiting. In the moment that he recognized this, a revelation came to him,—the knowledge that his horizon had been very narrow, and he felt angry that it was so. Why should those fellows be different from him? Why should they walk the streets so knowingly, so independently, when he knew not whither to turn his steps? Well, he was in New York, and now he would learn. Some day some greenhorn from the South should stand at a window and look out envying him, as he passed, red-cravated, patent-leathered, intent on some goal. Was it not better, after all, that circumstances had forced them thither? Had it not been so, they might all have stayed home and stagnated. Well, thought he, it's an ill wind that blows nobody good, and somehow, with a guilty under-thought, he forgot to feel the natural pity for his father, toiling guiltless in the prison of his native State.

Whom the Gods wish to destroy they first make mad. The first sign of the demoralization of the provincial who comes to New York is his pride at his insensibility to certain impressions which used to influence him at home. First, he begins to scoff, and there is no truth in his views nor depth in his laugh. But by and by, from mere pretending, it becomes real. He grows callous. After that he goes to the devil very cheerfully.

No such radical emotions, however, troubled Kit's mind. She too stood at the windows and looked down into the street. There was a sort of complacent calm in the manner in which she viewed the girls' hats and dresses. Many of them were really pretty, she told herself, but for the most part they were not better than what she had down home. There was a sound quality in the girl's make-up that helped her to see through the glamour of mere place and recognise worth for itself. Or it may have been the critical faculty, which is prominent in most women, that kept her from thinking a five-cent cheese-cloth any better in New York than it was at home. She had a certain self-respect which made her value herself and her own traditions higher than her brother did his.

When later in the evening the porter who had been kind to them came in and was introduced as Mr. William Thomas, young as she was, she took his open admiration for her with more coolness than Joe exhibited when Thomas offered to show him something of the town some day or night.

Mr. Thomas was a loquacious little man with a confident air born of an intense admiration of himself. He was the idol of a number of servant-girls' hearts, and altogether a decidedly dashing back-area-way Don Juan.

"I tell you, Miss Kitty," he burst forth, a few minutes after being introduced, "they ain't no use talkin', N' Yawk'll give you a shakin' up 'at you won't soon forget. It's the only town on the face of the earth. You kin bet your life they ain't no flies on N' Yawk. We git the best shows here, we git the best concerts—say now, what's the use o' my callin' it all out?—we simply git the best of everything."

"Great place," said Joe wisely, in what he thought was going to be quite a man-of-the-world manner. But he burned with shame the next minute because his voice sounded so weak and youthful. Then too the oracle only said "Yes" to him, and went on expatiating to Kitty on the glories of the metropolis.

"D' jever see the Statue o' Liberty? Great thing, the Statue o' Liberty. I'll take you 'round some day. An' Cooney Island—oh, my, now that's the place; and talk about fun! That's the place for me."

"La, Thomas," Mrs. Jones put in, "how you do run on! Why, the strangers'll think they'll be talked to death before they have time to breathe."

"Oh, I guess the folks understan' me. I'm one o' them kin' o' men 'at believe in whooping things up right from the beginning. I'm never strange with anybody. I'm a N' Yawker, I'll tell you, from the word go. I say, Mis' Jones, let's have some beer, an' we'll have some music purty soon. There's a fellah in the house 'at plays 'Rag-time' out o' sight."

Mr. Thomas took the pail and went to the corner. As he left the room, Mrs. Jones slapped her knee and laughed until her bust shook like jelly.

"Mr. Thomas is a case, sho'," she said; "but he likes

you all, an' I'm mighty glad of it, fu' he's mighty curious about the house when he don't like the roomers."

Joe felt distinctly flattered, for he found their new acquaintance charming. His mother was still a little doubtful, and Kitty was sure she found the young man "fresh."

He came in pretty soon with his beer, and a half-dozen crabs in a bag.

"Thought I'd bring home something to chew. I always like to eat something with my beer."

Mrs. Jones brought in the glasses, and the young man filled one and turned to Kitty.

"No, thanks," she said with a surprised look.

"What, don't you drink beer? Oh, come now, you'll get out o' that."

"Kitty don't drink no beer," broke in her mother with mild resentment. "I drinks it sometimes, but she don't. I reckon maybe de chillen better go to bed."

Joe felt as if the "chillen" had ruined all his hopes, but Kitty rose.

The ingratiating "N' Yawker" was aghast.

"Oh, let 'em stay," said Mrs. Jones heartily; "a little beer ain't goin' to hurt 'em. Why, sakes, I know my father gave me beer from the time I could drink it, and I knows I ain't none the worse fu' it."

"They'll git out o' that, all right, if they live in N' Yawk," said Mr. Thomas, as he poured out a glass and handed it to Joe. "You neither?"

"Oh, I drink it," said the boy with an air, but not looking at his mother.

"Joe," she cried to him, "you must ricollect you ain't at home. What 'ud yo' pa think?" Then she stopped suddenly, and Joe gulped his beer and Kitty went to the piano to relieve her embarrassment.

"Yes, that's it, Miss Kitty, sing us something," said the

irrepressible Thomas, "an' after while we'll have that fellah down that plays 'Rag-time.' He's out o' sight, I tell
you."

With the pretty shyness of girlhood, Kitty sang one
or two little songs in the simple manner she knew. Her
voice was full and rich. It delighted Mr. Thomas.

"I say, that's singin' now, I tell you," he cried. "You
ought to have some o' the new songs. D' jever hear
'Baby, you got to leave'? I tell you, that's a hot one. I'll
bring you some of 'em. Why, you could git a job on the
stage easy with that voice o' yourn. I got a frien' in one
o' the comp'nies an' I'll speak to him about you."

"You ought to git Mr. Thomas to take you to the
th'atre some night. He goes lots."

"Why, yes, what's the matter with to-morrer night?
There's a good coon show in town. Out o' sight. Let's
all go."

"I ain't nevah been to nothin' lak dat, an' I don't
know," said Mrs. Hamilton.

"Aw, come, I'll git the tickets an' we'll all go. Great
singin', you know. Whatd' you say?"

The mother hesitated, and Joe filled the breach.

"We'd all like to go," he said. "Ma, we'll go if you ain't
too tired."

"Tired? Pshaw, you'll furgit all about your tiredness
when Smithkins gits on the stage. Y' ought to hear him
sing, 'I bin huntin' fu' wo'k'! You'd die laughing."

Mrs. Hamilton made no further demur, and the matter was closed.

A while later the "Rag-time" man came down and
gave them a sample of what they were to hear the next
night. Mr. Thomas and Mrs. Jones two-stepped, and they
sent a boy after some more beer. Joe found it a very jolly

evening, but Kit's and the mother's hearts were heavy as they went up to bed.

"Say," said Mr. Thomas when they had gone, "that little girl's a peach, you bet; a little green, I guess, but she'll ripen in the sun."

CHAPTER 8

An Evening Out

FANNIE HAMILTON, tired as she was, sat long into the night with her little family discussing New York,—its advantages and disadvantages, its beauty and its ugliness, its morality and immorality. She had somewhat receded from her first position, that it was better being here in the great strange city than being at home where the very streets shamed them. She had not liked the way that their fellow lodger looked at Kitty. It was bold, to say the least. She was not pleased, either, with their new acquaintance's familiarity. And yet, he had said no more than some stranger, if there could be such a stranger, would have said down home. There was a difference, however, which she recognized. Thomas was not the provincial who puts every one on a par with himself, nor was he the metropolitan who complacently patronises the whole world. He was trained out of the one and not up to the other. The intermediate only succeeded in being offensive. Mrs. Jones's assurance as to her guest's fine qualities did not do all that might have been expected to reassure Mrs. Hamilton in the face of the difficulties of the gentleman's manner.

She could not, however, lay her finger on any particular point that would give her the reason for rejecting his friendly advances. She got ready the next evening to go to the theatre with the rest. Mr. Thomas at once possessed himself of Kitty and walked on ahead, leaving Joe to accompany his mother and Mrs. Jones,—an arrangement, by the way, not altogether to that young gentleman's taste. A good many men bowed to Thomas in the street, and they turned to look enviously after him. At the door of the theatre they had to run the gantlet of a dozen pairs of eyes. Here, too, the party's guide seemed to be well known, for some one said, before they passed out of hearing, "I wonder who that little light girl is that Thomas is with tonight. He's a hot one for you."

Mrs. Hamilton had been in a theatre but once before in her life, and Joe and Kit but a few times oftener. On those occasions they had sat far up in the peanut gallery in the place reserved for people of colour. This was not a pleasant, cleanly, nor beautiful locality, and by contrast with it, even the garishness of the cheap New York theatre seemed fine and glorious.

They had good seats in the first balcony, and here their guide had shown his managerial ability again, for he had found it impossible, or said so, to get all the seats together, so that he and the girl were in the row in front and to one side of where the rest sat. Kitty did not like the arrangement, and innocently suggested that her brother take her seat while she went back to her mother. But her escort overruled her objections easily, and laughed at her so frankly that from very shame she could not urge them again, and they were soon forgotten in her wonder at the mystery and glamour that envelops the home of the drama. There was something weird to her in the alternate spaces of light and shade. Without any feeling of its ugliness, she looked at the curtain as at a door that should presently open between her and a house of wonders. She looked at it with the fascination that one always experiences for what either brings near or withholds the unknown.

[As for Joe, he was not bothered by the mystery or the glamour of things. But he had suddenly raised himself in his own estimation. He had gazed steadily at a girl across the aisle until she had smiled in response. Of course, he went hot and cold by turns, and the sweat broke out on his brow, but instantly he began to swell. He had made a decided advance in knowledge, and he swelled with the consciousness that already he was coming to be a man of the world.] He looked with a new feeling at the swaggering, sporty young negroes. His attitude towards them was not one of humble self-deprecation any more. Since last night he had grown, and felt that he might, that he would, be like them, and it put a sort of chuckling glee into his heart.

One might find it in him to feel sorry for this small-souled, warped being, for he was so evidently the jest of Fate, if it were not that he was so blissfully, so conceitedly, unconscious of his own nastiness. Down home he had shaved the wild young bucks of the town, and while doing it drunk in eagerly their unguarded narrations of their gay exploits. So he had started out with false ideals as to what was fine and manly. He was afflicted by a sort of moral and mental astigmatism that made him see everything wrong. As he sat there tonight, he gave to all he saw a wrong value and upon it based his ignorant desires.

When the men of the orchestra filed in and began tuning their instruments, it was the signal for an influx of loiterers from the door. There was a large number of coloured people in the audience, and because members of their own race were giving the performance, they seemed to take a proprietary interest in it all. They discussed its merits and demerits as they walked down the aisle in much the same tone that the owners would have used had they been wondering whether the entertainment was going to please the people or not.

Finally the music struck up one of the numerous negro marches. It was accompanied by the rhythmic patting of feet from all parts of the house. Then the curtain went up on a scene of beauty. It purported to be a grove to which a party of picnickers, the ladies and gentlemen of the chorus, had come for a holiday, and they were telling the audience all about it in crescendos. With the exception of one, who looked like a faded kid glove, the men discarded the grease paint, but the women under their make-ups ranged from pure white, pale yellow, and sickly greens to brick reds and slate grays. They were dressed in costumes that were not primarily intended for picnic going. But they could sing, and they did sing, with their voices, their bodies, their souls. They threw themselves into it because they enjoyed and felt what they were doing, and they gave almost a semblance of dignity to the tawdry music and inane words.

Kitty was enchanted. The airily dressed women seemed to her like creatures from fairy-land. It is strange how the glare of the footlights succeeds in deceiving so many people who are able to see through other delusions. The cheap dresses on the street had not fooled Kitty for an instant, but take the same cheese-cloth, put a little water starch into it, and put it on the stage, and she could see only chiffon.

She turned around and nodded delightedly at her brother, but he did not see her. He was lost, transfixed. His soul was floating on a sea of sense. He had eyes and

ears and thoughts only for the stage. His nerves tingled
and his hands twitched. Only to know one of those radi
ant creatures, to have her speak to him, smile at him
If ever a man was intoxicated, Joe was. Mrs. Hamilton
was divided between shame at the clothes of some of
the women and delight with the music. Her companion
was busy pointing out who this and that actress was, and
giving jelly-like appreciation to the doings on the stage.

Mr. Thomas was the only cool one in the party. He
was quietly taking stock of his young companion,—of
her innocence and charm. She was a pretty girl, little and
dainty, but well developed for her age. Her hair was very
black and wavy, and some strain of the South's chivalric
blood, which is so curiously mingled with the African in
the veins of most coloured people, had tinged her skin
to an olive hue.

"Are you enjoying yourself?" he leaned over and
whispered to her. His voice was very confidential and
his lips near her ear, but she did not notice.

"Oh, yes," she answered, "this is grand. How I'd like
to be an actress and be up there!"

"Maybe you will some day."

"Oh, no, I'm not smart enough."

"We'll see," he said wisely; "I know a thing or two."

Between the first and second acts a number of
Thomas's friends strolled up to where he sat and began
talking, and again Kitty's embarrassment took possession of her as they were introduced one by one. They
treated her with a half-courteous familiarity that made
her blush. Her mother was not pleased with the many
acquaintances that her daughter was making, and would
have interfered had not Mrs. Jones assured her that the
men clustered about their host's seat were some of the
"best people in town." Joe looked at them hungrily, but

the man in front with his sister did not think it necessary to include the brother or the rest of the party in his miscellaneous introductions.

One brief bit of conversation which the mother overheard especially troubled her.

"Not going out for a minute or two?" asked one of the men, as he was turning away from Thomas.

"No, I don't think I'll go out to-night. You can have my share."

The fellow gave a horse laugh and replied, "Well, you're doing a great piece of work, Miss Hamilton, whenever you can keep old Bill from goin' out an' lushin' between acts. Say, you got a good thing; push it along."

The girl's mother half rose, but she resumed her seat, for the man was going away. Her mind was not quiet again, however, until the people were all in their seats and the curtain had gone up on the second act. At first she was surprised at the enthusiasm over just such dancing as she could see any day from the loafers on the street corners down home, and then, like a good, sensible, humble woman, she came around to the idea that it was she who had always been wrong in putting too low a value on really worthy things. So she laughed and applauded with the rest, all the while trying to quiet something that was tugging at her way down in her heart.

When the performance was over she forced her way to Kitty's side, where she remained in spite of all Thomas's palpable efforts to get her away. Finally he proposed that they all go to supper at one of the coloured cafés.

"You'll see a lot o' the show people," he said.

"No, I reckon we'd bettah go home," said Mrs. Hamilton decidedly. "De chillen ain't ust to stayin' up all hours o' nights, an' I ain't anxious fu' 'em to git ust to it."

She was conscious of a growing dislike for this man

who treated her daughter with such a proprietary air. Joe winced again at "de chillen."

Thomas bit his lip, and mentally said things that are unfit for publication. Aloud he said, "Mebbe Miss Kitty'ud like to go an' have a little lunch."

"Oh, no, thank you," said the girl; "I've had a nice time and I don't care for a thing to eat."

Joe told himself that Kitty was the biggest fool that it had ever been his lot to meet, and the disappointed suitor satisfied himself with the reflection that the girl was green yet, but would get bravely over that.

He attempted to hold her hand as they parted at the parlour door, but she drew her fingers out of his clasp and said, "Good-night; thank you," as if he had been one of her mother's old friends.

Joe lingered a little longer.

"Say, that was out o' sight," he said.

"Think so?" asked the other carelessly.

"I'd like to get out with you some time to see the town," the boy went on eagerly.

"All right, we'll go some time. So long."

"So long."

Some time. Was it true? Would he really take him out and let him meet stage people? Joe went to bed with his head in a whirl. He slept little that night for thinking of his heart's desire.

CHAPTER 9

His Heart's Desire

WHATEVER ELSE HIS VISIT to the theatre may have done for Joe, it inspired him with a desire to go to work and earn money of his own, to be independent both of parental help and control, and so be able to spend as he pleased. With this end in view he set out to hunt for work. It was a pleasant contrast to his last similar quest, and he felt it with joy. He was treated everywhere he went with courtesy, even when no situation was forthcoming. Finally he came upon a man who was willing to try him for an afternoon. From the moment the boy rightly considered himself engaged, for he was master of his trade. He began his work with heart elate. Now he had within his grasp the possibility of being all that he wanted to be. Now Thomas might take him out at any time and not be ashamed of him.

With Thomas, the fact that Joe was working put the boy in an entirely new light. He decided that now he might be worth cultivating. For a week or two he had ignored him, and, proceeding upon the principle that if you give corn to the old hen she will cluck to her chicks, had treated Mrs. Hamilton with marked deference and kindness. This had been without success, as both the girl and her mother held themselves politely aloof from him. He began to see that his hope of winning Kitty's affections lay, not in courting the older woman but in making a friend of the boy. So on a certain Saturday night when the Banner Club was to give one of its smokers, he asked Joe to go with him. Joe was glad to, and they set out together. Arrived, Thomas left his companion for a few moments while he attended, as he said, to a little business. What he really did was seek out the proprietor of the club and some of its hangers on.

"I say," he said, "I've got a friend with me to-night. He's got some dough on him. He's fresh and young and easy."

"Whew!" exclaimed the proprietor.

"Yes, he's a good thing, but push it along kin' o' light at first; he might get skittish."

"Thomas, let me fall on your bosom and weep," said a young man who, on account of his usual expression of innocent gloom, was called Sadness. "This is what I've been looking for for a month. My hat was getting decidedly shabby. Do you think he would stand for a touch on the first night of our acquaintance?"

"Don't you dare! Do you want to frighten him off? Make him believe that you've got coin to burn and that it's an honour to be with you."

"But, you know, he may expect a glimpse of the gold."

"A smart man don't need to show nothin'. All he's got to do is to act."

"Oh, I'll act; we'll all act."

"Be slow to take a drink from him."

"Thomas, my boy, you're an angel. I recognise that more and more every day, but bid me do anything else but that. That I refuse: it's against nature"; and Sadness looked more mournful than ever.

"Trust old Sadness to do his part," said the portly proprietor; and Thomas went back to the lamb.

"Nothin' doin' so early," he said; "let's go an' have a drink."

They went, and Thomas ordered.

"No, no, this is on me," cried Joe, trembling with joy.

"Pshaw, your money's counterfeit," said his companion with fine generosity. "This is on me, I say. Jack, what'll you have yourself?"

As they stood at the bar, the men began strolling up one by one. Each in his turn was introduced to Joe. They were very polite. They treated him with a pale, dignified, high-minded respect that menaced his pocket-book and possessions. The proprietor, Mr. Turner, asked him why he had never been in before. He really seemed much hurt about it, and on being told that Joe had only been in the city for a couple of weeks expressed emphatic surprise, even disbelief, and assured the rest that any one would have taken Mr. Hamilton for an old New Yorker.

Sadness was introduced last. He bowed to Joe's "Happy to know you, Mr. Williams."

"Better known as Sadness," he said, with an expression of deep gloom. "A distant relative of mine once had a great grief. I have never recovered from it."

Joe was not quite sure how to take this; but the others laughed and he joined them, and then, to cover his own embarrassment, he did what he thought the only correct and manly thing to do,—he ordered a drink.

"I don't know as I ought to," said Sadness.

"Oh, come on," his companions called out, "don't be stiff with a stranger. Make him feel at home."

"Mr. Hamilton will believe me when I say that I have no intention of being stiff, but duty is duty. I've got to go down town to pay a bill, and if I get too much aboard, it wouldn't be safe walking around with money on me."

"Aw, shut up, Sadness," said Thomas. "My friend Mr. Hamilton 'll feel hurt if you don't drink with him."

"I cert'n'y will," was Joe's opportune remark, and he was pleased to see that it caused the reluctant one to yield.

They took a drink. There was quite a line of them. Joe asked the bartender what he would have. The men warmed towards him. They took several more drinks with him and he was happy. Sadness put his arm about his shoulder and told him, with tears in his eyes, that he looked like a cousin of his that had died.

"Aw, shut up, Sadness!" said someone else. "Be respectable."

Sadness turned his mournful eyes upon the speaker. "I won't," he replied. "Being respectable is very nice as a diversion, but it's tedious if done steadily." Joe did not quite take this, so he ordered another drink.

A group of young fellows came in and passed up the stairs. "Shearing another lamb?" said one of them significantly.

"Well, with that gang it will be well done."

Thomas and Joe left the crowd after a while, and went to the upper floor, where, in a long, brilliantly lighted room, tables were set out for drinking-parties. At one end of the room was a piano, and a man sat at it listlessly strumming some popular air. The proprietor joined them pretty soon, and steered them to a table opposite the door.

"Just sit down here, Mr. Hamilton," he said, "and you can see everybody that comes in. We have lots of nice people here on smoker nights, especially after the shows are out and the girls come in."

Joe's heart gave a great leap, and then settled as cold as lead. Of course, those girls wouldn't speak to him. But his hopes rose as the proprietor went on talking to him and to no one else. Mr. Turner always made a man feel as if he were of some consequence in the world, and men a good deal older than Joe had been fooled by his manner. He talked to one in a soft, ingratiating way, giving his whole attention apparently. He tapped one confidentially on the shoulder, as who should say, "My dear boy, I have but two friends in the world, and you are both of them."

Joe, charmed and pleased, kept his head well. There is a great deal in heredity, and his father had not been Maurice Oakley's butler for so many years for nothing.

The Banner Club was an institution for the lower education of negro youth. It drew its pupils from every class of people and from every part of the country. It was composed of all sorts and conditions of men, educated and uneducated, dishonest and less so, of the good, the bad, and the—unexposed. Parasites came there to find victims, politicians for votes, reporters for news, and artists of all kinds for colour and inspiration. It was the place of assembly for a number of really bright men, who after days of hard and often unrewarded work came there and drank themselves drunk in each other's company, and when they were drunk talked of the eternal verities.

The Banner was only one of a kind. It stood to the stranger and the man and woman without connections for the whole social life. It was a substitute—poor, it must be confessed—to many youths for the home life which is so lacking among certain classes in New York.

Here the rounders congregated, or came and spent the hours until it was time to go forth to bout or assignation. Here too came sometimes the curious who wanted to see something of the other side of life. Among these, white visitors were not infrequent,—those who were young enough to be fascinated by the bizarre, and those who were old enough to know that it was all in the game. Mr. Skaggs, of the New York *Universe*, was one of the former class and a constant visitor,—he and a "lady friend" called "Maudie," who had a penchant for dancing to "Rag-time" melodies as only the "puffessor" of such a club can play them. Of course, the place was a social cesspool, generating a poisonous miasma and reeking with the stench of decayed and rotten moralities. There is no defense to be made for it. But what do you expect when false idealism and fevered ambition come face to face with catering cupidity?

It was into this atmosphere that Thomas had introduced the boy Joe, and he sat there now by his side, firing his mind by pointing out the different celebrities who came in and telling highly flavoured stories of their lives or doings. Joe heard things that had never come within the range of his mind before.

"Aw, there's Skaggsy an' Maudie—Maudie's his girl, y' know, an' he's a reporter on the N' Yawk *Universe*. Fine fellow, Skaggsy."

Maudie—a portly, voluptuous-looking brunette—left her escort and went directly to the space by the piano. Here she was soon dancing with one of the coloured girls who had come in.

Skaggs started to sit down alone at a table, but Thomas called him, "Come over here, Skaggsy."

In the moment that it took the young man to reach them, Joe wondered if he would ever reach that state when he could call that white man Skaggsy and the girl Maudie. The new-comer set all of that at ease.

"I want you to know my friend, Mr. Hamilton, Mr. Skaggs."

"Why, how d' ye do, Hamilton? I'm glad to meet you. Now, look a here; don't you let old Thomas here string you about me bein' any old 'Mr!' Skaggs. I'm Skaggsy to all of my friends. I hope to count you among 'em."

It was such a supreme moment that Joe could not find words to answer, so he called for another drink.

"Not a bit of it," said Skaggsy, "not a bit of it. When I meet my friends I always reserve to myself the right of ordering the first drink. Waiter, this is on me. What'll you have, gentlemen?"

They got their drinks, and then Skaggsy leaned over confidentially and began talking.

"I tell you, Hamilton, there ain't an ounce of prejudice in my body. Do you believe it?"

Joe said that he did. Indeed Skaggsy struck one as being aggressively unprejudiced.

He went on: "You see, a lot o' fellows say to me, 'What do you want to go down to that nigger club for?' That's what they call it,—'nigger club.' But I say to 'em, 'Gentlemen, at that nigger club, as you choose to call it, I get more inspiration than I could get at any of the greater clubs in New York.' I've often been invited to join some of the swell clubs here, but I never do it. By Jove! I'd rather come down here and fellowship right in with you fellows. I like coloured people, anyway. It's natural. You see, my father had a big plantation and owned lots of slaves,—no offense, of course, but it was the custom of that time,—and I've played with little darkies ever since I could remember."

It was the same old story that the white who associates with negroes from volition usually tells to explain his taste.

The truth about the young reporter was that he was born and reared on a Vermont farm, where his early life was passed in fighting for his very subsistence. But this never troubled Skaggsy. He was a monumental liar, and the saving quality about him was that he calmly believed his own lies while he was telling them, so no one was hurt, for the deceiver was as much a victim as the deceived. The boys who knew him best used to say that when Skaggs got started on one of his debauches of lying, the Recording Angel always put on an extra clerical force.

"Now look at Maudie," he went on; "would you believe it that she was of a fine, rich family, and that the coloured girl she's dancing with now used to be her servant? She's just like me about that. Absolutely no prejudice."

Joe was wide-eyed with wonder and admiration, and he couldn't understand the amused expression on Thomas's face, nor why he surreptitiously kicked him under the table.

Finally the reporter went his way, and Joe's sponsor explained to him that he was not to take in what Skaggsy said, and that there hadn't been a word of truth in it. He ended with, "everybody knows Maudie, and that coloured girl is Mamie Lacey, and never worked for anybody in her life. Skaggsy's a good fellah, all right, but he's the biggest liar in N' Yawk."

The boy was distinctly shocked. He wasn't sure but Thomas was jealous of the attention the white man had shown him and wished to belittle it. Anyway, he did not thank him for destroying his romance.

About eleven o'clock, when the people began to drop in from the plays, the master of ceremonies opened proceedings by saying that "The free concert would now begin, and he hoped that all present, ladies included, would act like gentlemen, and not forget the waiter. Mr. Meriweather will now favour us with the latest coon song, entitled 'Come back to yo' Baby, Honey.' "

There was a patter of applause, and a young negro came forward, and in a strident, music-hall voice, sung or rather recited with many gestures the ditty. He couldn't have been much older than Joe, but already his face was hard with dissipation and foul knowledge. He gave the song with all the rank suggestiveness that could be put into it. Joe looked upon him as a hero. He was followed by a little, brown-skinned fellow with an immature Vandyke beard and a lisp. He sung his own composition and was funny; how much funnier than he himself knew or intended, may not even be hinted at. Then, while an instrumentalist, who seemed to have a grudge against the piano, was hammering out the open-ing bars of a march, Joe's attention was attracted by a woman entering the room, and from that moment he heard no more of the concert. Even when the master of ceremonies announced with an air that, by special request, he himself would sing "Answer,"—the request was his own,—he did not draw the attention of the boy away from the yellow-skinned divinity who sat at a near table, drinking whiskey straight.

She was a small girl, with fluffy dark hair and good features. A tiny foot peeped out from beneath her rat-tling silk skirts. She was a good-looking young woman and daintily made, though her face was no longer youth-ful, and one might have wished that with her complex-ion she had not run to silk waists in magenta.

Joe, however, saw no fault in her. She was altogether lovely to him, and his delight was the more poignant as he recognized in her one of the girls he had seen on the stage a couple of weeks ago. That being true, nothing could keep her from being glorious in his eyes,—not even the grease-paint which adhered in unneat patches to her face, nor her taste for whiskey in its unreformed state. He gazed at her in ecstasy until Thomas, turning to see what had attracted him, said with a laugh, "Oh, it's Hattie Sterling. Want to meet her?"

Again the young fellow was dumb. Just then Hattie also noticed his intent look, and nodded and beckoned to Thomas.

"Come on," he said, rising.

"Oh, she didn't ask for me," cried Joe, tremulous and eager.

His companion went away laughing.

"Who's your young friend?" asked Hattie.

"A fella from the South."

"Bring him over here."

Joe could hardly believe in his own good luck, and his head, which was getting a bit weak, was near collapsing when his divinity asked him what he'd have. He began to protest, until she told the waiter with an air of authority to make it a little " 'skey." Then she asked him for a cigarette, and began talking to him in a pleasant, soothing way between puffs.

When the drinks came, she said to Thomas, "Now, old man, you've been awfully nice, but when you get your little drink, you run away like a good little boy. You're superfluous."

Thomas answered, "Well, I like that," but obediently gulped his whiskey and withdrew, while Joe laughed until the master of ceremonies stood up and looked sternly at him.

The concert had long been over and the room was less crowded when Thomas sauntered back to the pair.

"Well, good-night," he said. "Guess you can find your way home, Mr. Hamilton"; and he gave Joe a long wink.

"Goo'-night," said Joe, woozily, "I be a' ri'. Goo'-night."

"Make it another 'skey," was Hattie's farewell remark.

It was late the next morning when Joe got home. He had a headache and a sense of triumph that not even his illness and his mother's reproof could subdue.

He had promised Hattie to come often to the club.

CHAPTER 10

A Visitor from Home

MRS. HAMILTON BEGAN to question very seriously whether she had done the best thing in coming to New York as she saw her son staying away more and more and growing always farther away from her and his sister. Had she known how and where he spent his·evenings, she would have had even greater cause to question the wisdom of their trip. She knew that although he worked he never had any money for the house, and she foresaw the time when the little they had would no longer suffice for Kitty and her. Realising this, she herself set out to find something to do.

It was a hard matter, for wherever she went seeking employment, it was always for her and her daughter, for the more she saw of Mrs. Jones, the less she thought it well to leave the girl under her influence. Mrs. Hamilton was not a keen woman, but she had a mother's intuitions, and she saw a subtle change in her daughter. At first the girl grew wistful and then impatient and rebellious. She complained that Joe was away from them so much enjoying himself, while she had to be housed up like a prisoner. She had receded from her dignified position, and twice of an evening had gone out for a car-ride with Thomas; but as that gentleman never included the mother in his invitation, she decided that her daughter should go no more, and she begged Joe to take his sister out sometimes instead. He demurred at first, for he now numbered among his city acquirements a fine contempt for his woman relatives. Finally, however, he consented, and took Kit once to the theatre and once for a ride. Each time he left her in the care of Thomas as soon as they were out of the house, while he went to find or to wait for his dear Hattie. But his mother did not know all this, and Kit did not tell her. The quick poison of the unreal life about her had already begun to affect her character. She had grown secretive and sly. The innocent longing which in a burst of enthusiasm she had expressed that first night at the theatre was growing into a real ambition with her, and she dropped the simple old songs she knew to practise the detestable coon ditties which the stage demanded.

She showed no particular pleasure when her mother found the sort of place they wanted, but went to work with her in sullen silence. Mrs. Hamilton could not understand it all, and many a night she wept and prayed over the change in this child of her heart. There were times when she felt that there was nothing left to work or fight for. The letters from Berry in prison became fewer and fewer. He was sinking into the dull, dead routine of his life. Her own letters to him fell off. It was hard getting the children to write. They did not want to be bothered, and she could not write for herself. So in the weeks and months that followed she drifted farther away from her children and husband and all the traditions of her life.

After Joe's first night at the Banner Club he had kept his promise to Hattie Sterling and had gone often to meet her. She had taught him much, because it was to her advantage to do so. His greenness had dropped from him like a garment, but no amount of sophistication could make him deem the woman less perfect. He knew that she was much older than he, but he only took this fact as an additional sign of his prowess in having won her. He was proud of himself when he went behind the scenes at the theatre or waited for her at the stage door and bore her off under the admiring eyes of a crowd of gapers. And Hattie? She liked him in a half-contemptuous, half-amused way. He was a good-looking boy and made money enough, as she expressed it, to show her a good time, so she was willing to overlook his weakness and his callow vanity.

"Look here," she said to him one day. "I guess you'll have to be moving. There's a young lady been inquiring for you to-day, and I won't stand for that."

He looked at her, startled for a moment, until he saw the laughter in her eyes. Then he caught her and kissed her. "What're you givin' me?" he said.

"It's a straight tip, that's what."

"Who is it?"

"It's a girl named Minty Brown from your home."

His face turned brick-red with fear and shame. "Minty Brown!" he stammered.

Had that girl told all and undone him? But Hattie was going on about her work and evidently knew nothing.

"Oh, you needn't pretend you don't know her," she went on banteringly. "She says you were great friends down South, so I've invited her to supper. She wants to see you."

"To supper!" he thought. Was she mocking him? Was she restraining her scorn of him only to make his humiliation the greater after a while? He looked at her, but there was no suspicion of malice in her face, and he took hope.

"Well, I'd like to see old Minty," he said. "It's been many a long day since I've seen her."

All that afternoon, after going to the barber-shop, Joe was driven by a tempest of conflicting emotions. If Minty Brown had not told his story, why not? Would she yet tell, and if she did, what would happen? He tortured himself by questioning if Hattie would cast him off. At the very thought his hand trembled, and the man in the chair asked him if he hadn't been drinking.

When he met Minty in the evening, however, the first glance at her reassured him. Her face was wreathed in smiles as she came forward and held out her hand.

"Well, well, Joe Hamilton," she exclaimed, "if I ain't right-down glad to see you! How are you?"

"I'm middlin', Minty. How's yourself?" He was so happy that he couldn't let go of her hand.

"An' jes' look at the boy! Ef he ain't got the impidence to be waihin' a mustache too. You must 'a' been lettin' the cats lick yo' upper lip. Didn't expect to see me in New York, did you?"

"No, indeed. What you doin' here?"

"Oh, I got a gent'man friend what's a porter, an' his run's been changed so that he comes hyeah, an' he told me, if I wanted to come he'd bring me thoo fur a visit, so, you see, hyeah I am. I allus was mighty anxious to see this hyeah town. But tell me, how's Kit an' yo' ma?"

"They're both right well." He had forgotten them and their scorn of Minty.

"Whaih do you live? I'm comin' roun' to see 'em."

He hesitated for a moment. He knew how his mother, if not Kit, would receive her, and yet he dared not anger this woman, who had his fate in the hollow of her hand.

She saw his hesitation and spoke up. "Oh, that's all right. Let by-gones be by-gones. You know I ain't the kin' o' person that holds a grudge ag'in anybody."

"That's right, Minty, that's right," he said, and gave her his mother's address. Then he hastened home to prepare the way for Minty's coming. Joe had no doubt but that his mother would see the matter quite as he saw it, and be willing to temporise with Minty; but he had reckoned without his host. Mrs. Hamilton might make certain concessions to strangers on the score of expediency, but she absolutely refused to yield one iota of her dignity to one whom she had known so long as an inferior.

"But don't you see what she can do for us, ma? She knows people that I know, and she can ruin me with them."

"I ain't never bowed my haid to Minty Brown an' I ain't a-goin' to do it now," was his mother's only reply.

"Oh, ma," Kitty put in, "you don't want to get talked about up here, do you?"

"We'd jes' as well be talked about fu' somep'n we didn't do as fu' somep'n we did do, an' it wouldn' be long befo' we'd come to dat if we made frien's wid dat Brown gal. I ain't a-goin' to do it. I'm ashamed o' you, Kitty, fu' wantin' me to."

The girl began to cry, while her brother walked the floor angrily.

"You'll see what'll happen," he cried; "you'll see."

Fannie looked at her son, and she seemed to see him more clearly than she had ever seen him before,—his foppery, his meanness, his cowardice.

"Well," she answered with a sigh, "it can't be no wuss den what's already happened."

"You'll see, you'll see," the boy reiterated.

Minty Brown allowed no wind of thought to cool the fire of her determination. She left Hattie Sterling's soon after Joe, and he was still walking the floor and uttering dire forebodings when she rang the bell below and asked for the Hamiltons.

Mrs. Jones ushered her into her fearfully upholstered parlour, and then puffed up stairs to tell her lodgers that there was a friend there from the South who wanted to see them.

"Tell huh," said Mrs. Hamilton, "dat dey ain't no one hyeah wants to see huh."

"No, no," Kitty broke in.

"Heish," said her mother; "I'm goin' to boss you a little while yit."

"Why, I don't understan' you, Mis' Hamilton," puffed Mrs. Jones. "She's a nice-lookin' lady, an' she said she knowed you at home."

"All you got to do is to tell dat ooman jes' what I say."

Minty Brown downstairs had heard the little colloquy, and, perceiving that something was amiss, had come to the stairs to listen. Now her voice, striving hard to be condescending and sweet, but growing harsh with anger, floated up from below:

"Oh, nevah min', lady. I ain't anxious to see 'em. I jest called out o' pity, but I reckon dey 'shamed to see me 'cause de ol' man's in penitentiary an' dey was run out o' town."

Mrs. Jones gasped, and then turned and went hastily downstairs.

Kit burst out crying afresh, and Joe walked the floor muttering beneath his breath, while the mother sat grimly watching the outcome. Finally they heard Mrs. Jones's step once more on the stairs. She came in without knocking, and her manner was distinctly unpleasant.

"Mis' Hamilton," she said, "I've had a talk with the lady downstairs, an' she's tol' me everything. I'd be glad if you'd let me have my rooms as soon as possible."

"So you goin' to put me out on de wo'd of a stranger?"

"I'm kin' o' sorry, but everybody in the house heard what Mis' Brown said, an' it'll soon be all over town, an' that 'ud ruin the reputation of my house."

"I reckon all dat kin be 'splained."

"Yes, but I don't know that anybody kin 'splain your daughter allus being with Mr. Thomas, who ain't even divo'ced from his wife." She flashed a vindictive glance at the girl, who turned deadly pale and dropped her head in her hands.

"You daih to say dat, Mis' Jones, you dat fust inter-duced my gal to dat man and got huh to go out wid him? I reckon you'd bettah go now."

And Mrs. Jones looked at Fannie's face and obeyed.

As soon as the woman's back was turned, Joe burst out, "There, there! see what you've done with your damned foolishness."

Fannie turned on him like a tigress. "Don't you cuss hyeah befo' me; I ain't nevah brung you up to it, an' I won't stan' it. Go to dem whaih you larned it, an whaih de wo'ds soun' sweet." The boy started to speak, but she checked him. "Don't you daih to cuss ag'in or befo' Gawd dey'll be somep'n fu' one o' dis fambly to be rot-tin' in jail fu'!"

The boy was cowed by his mother's manner. He was gathering his few belongings in a bundle.

"I ain't goin' to cuss," he said sullenly. "I'm goin' out o' your way."

"Oh, go on," she said, "go on. It's been a long time sence you been my son. You on yo' way to hell, an' you is been fu' lo dese many days."

Joe got out of the house as soon as possible. He did not speak to Kit nor look at his mother. He felt like a cur, because he knew deep down in his heart that he had only been waiting for some excuse to take this step.

As he slammed the door behind him, his mother flung herself down by Kit's side and mingled her tears with her daughter's. But Kit did not raise her head.

"Dey ain't nothin' lef' but you now, Kit"; but the girl did not speak; she only shook with hard sobs.

Then her mother raised her head and almost screamed, "My Gawd, not you, Kit!" The girl rose, and then dropped unconscious in her mother's arms.

Joe took his clothes to a lodging-house that he knew of, and then went to the club to drink himself up to the point of going to see Hattie after the show.

CHAPTER 11

Broken Hopes

WHAT JOE HAMILTON lacked more than anything else in the world was some one to kick him. Many a man who might have lived decently and become a fairly respectable citizen has gone to the dogs for the want of some one to administer a good resounding kick at the right time. It is corrective and clarifying.

Joe needed especially its clarifying property, for though he knew himself a cur, he went away from his mother's house feeling himself somehow aggrieved, and the feeling grew upon him the more he thought of it. His mother had ruined his chance in life, and he could never hold up his head again. Yes, he had heard that several of the fellows at the club had shady reputations, but surely to be the son of a thief or a supposed thief was not like being the criminal himself.

At the Banner he took a seat by himself, and, ordering a cocktail, sat glowering at the few other lonely members who had happened to drop in. There were not many of them, and the contagion of unsociability had taken possession of the house. The people sat scattered around at different tables, perfectly unmindful of the bartender, who cursed them under his breath for not "getting together."

Joe's mind was filled with bitter thoughts. How long had he been away from home? he asked himself. Nearly a year. Nearly a year passed in New York, and he had come to be what he so much desired,—a part of its fast life,—and now in a moment an old woman's stubbornness had destroyed all that he had builded.

What would Thomas say when he heard it? What would the other fellows think? And Hattie? It was plain that she would never notice him again. He had no doubt but that the malice of Minty Brown would prompt her to seek out all of his friends and make the story known. Why had he not tried to placate her by disavowing sympathy with his mother? He would have had no compunction about doing so, but he had thought of it too late. He sat brooding over his trouble until the bartender called with respectful sarcasm to ask if he wanted to lease the glass he had.

He gave back a silly laugh, gulped the rest of the liquor down, and was ordering another when Sadness came in. He came up directly to Joe and sat down beside him. "Mr. Hamilton says 'Make it two, Jack,'" he said with easy familiarity. "Well, what's the matter, old man? You're looking glum."

"I feel glum."

"The divine Hattie hasn't been cutting any capers, has she? The dear old girl hasn't been getting hysterical at her age? Let us hope not."

Joe glared at him. Why in the devil should this fellow be so sadly gay when he was weighted down with sorrow and shame and disgust?

"Come, come now, Hamilton. If you're sore because I

invited myself to take a drink with you, I'll withdraw the order. I know the heroic thing to say is that I'll pay for the drinks myself, but I can't screw my courage up to the point of doing so unnatural a thing."

Young Hamilton hastened to protest. "Oh, I know you fellows now well enough to know how many drinks to pay for. It ain't that."

"Well, then, out with it. What is it? Haven't been up to anything, have you?"

The desire came to Joe to tell this man the whole truth, just what was the matter, and so to relieve his heart. On the impulse he did. If he had expected much from Sadness he was disappointed, for not a muscle of the man's face changed during the entire recital.

When it was over, he looked at his companion critically through a wreath of smoke. Then he said: "For a fellow who has had for a full year the advantage of the education of the New York clubs, you are strangely young. Let me see, you are nineteen or twenty now— yes. Well, that perhaps accounts for it. It's a pity you weren't born older. It's a pity that most men aren't. They wouldn't have to take so much time and lose so many good things learning. Now, Mr. Hamilton, let me tell you, and you will pardon me for it, that you are a fool. Your case isn't half as bad as that of nine-tenths of the fellows that hang around here. Now, for instance, my father was hung."

Joe started and gave a gasp of horror.

"Oh yes, but it was done with a very good rope and by the best citizens of Texas, so it seems that I really ought to be very grateful to them for the distinction they conferred upon my family, but I am not. I am ungratefully sad. A man must be very high or very low to take the sensible view of life that keeps him from being sad. I must confess that I have aspired to the depths without ever being fully able to reach them.

"Now look around a bit. See that little girl over there? That's Viola. Two years ago she wrenched up an iron stool from the floor of a lunch-room, and killed another woman with it. She's nineteen,—just about your age, by the way. Well, she had friends with a certain amount of pull. She got out of it, and no one thinks the worse of Viola. You see, Hamilton, in this life we are all suffering from fever, and no one edges away from the other because he finds him a little warm. It's dangerous when you're not used to it; but once you go through the parching process, you become inoculated against further contagion. Now, there's Barney over there, as decent a fellow as I know; but he has been indicted twice for pocket-picking. A half-dozen fellows whom you meet here every night have killed their man. Others have done worse things for which you respect them less. Poor Wallace, who is just coming in, and who looks like a jaunty rag-picker, came here about six months ago with about two thousand dollars, the proceeds from the sale of a house his father had left him. He'll sleep in one of the club chairs to-night, and not from choice. He spent his two thousand learning. But, after all, it was a good investment. It was like buying an annuity. He begins to know already how to live on others as they have lived on him. The plucked bird's beak is sharpened for other's feathers. From now on Wallace will live, eat, drink, and sleep at the expense of others, and will forget to mourn his lost money. He will go on this way until, broken and useless, the poorhouse or the potter's field gets him. Oh, it's a fine, rich life, my lad. I know you'll like it. I said you would the first time I saw you. It has plenty of stir in it, and a man never gets lonesome. Only the rich are lonesome. It's only the independent who depend upon others."

Sadness laughed a peculiar laugh, and there was a look in his terribly bright eyes that made Joe creep. If he could only have understood all that the man was saying to him, he might even yet have turned back. But he didn't. He ordered another drink. The only effect that the talk of Sadness had upon him was to make him feel wonderfully "in it." It gave him a false bravery, and he mentally told himself that now he would not be afraid to face Hattie.

He put out his hand to Sadness with a knowing look. "Thanks, Sadness," he said, "you've helped me lots."

Sadness brushed the proffered hand away and sprung up. "You lie," he cried. "I haven't; I was only fool enough to try"; and he turned hastily away from the table.

Joe looked surprised at first, and then laughed at his friend's retreating form. "Poor old fellow," he said, "drunk again. Must have had something before he came in."

There was not a lie in all that Sadness had said either as to their crime or their condition. He belonged to a peculiar class,—one that grows larger and larger each year in New York and which has imitators in every large city in this country. It is a set which lives, like the leech, upon the blood of others,—that draws its life from the veins of foolish men and immoral women, that prides itself upon its well-dressed idleness and has no shame in its voluntary pauperism. Each member of the class knows every other, his methods and his limitations, and their loyalty one to another makes of them a great hulking, fashionably uniformed fraternity of indolence. Some play the races a few months of the year; others, quite as intermittently, gamble at "shoestring" politics, and waver from party to party as time or their interests seem to dictate. But mostly they are like the lilies of the field.

It was into this set that Sadness had sarcastically invited Joe, and Joe felt honored. He found that all of his former feelings had been silly and quite out of place; that all he had learned in his earlier years was false. It was very plain to him now that to want a good reputation was the sign of unpardonable immaturity, and that dishonor was the only real thing worthwhile. It made him feel better.

He was just rising bravely to swagger out to the theatre when Minty Brown came in with one of the clubmen he knew. He bowed and smiled, but she appeared not to notice him at first, and when she did she nudged her companion and laughed.

Suddenly his little courage began to ooze out, and he knew what she must be saying to the fellow at her side, for he looked over at him and grinned. Where now was the philosophy of Sadness? Evidently Minty had not been brought under its educating influences, and thought about the whole matter in the old, ignorant way. He began to think of it too. Somehow old teachings and old traditions have an annoying way of coming back upon us in the critical moments of life, although one has long ago recognised how much truer and better some newer ways of thinking are. But Joe would not allow Minty to shatter his dreams by bringing up these old notions. She must be instructed.

He rose and went over to her table.

"Why, Minty," he said, offering his hand, "you ain't mad at me, are you?"

"Go on away f'om hyeah," she said angrily; "I don't want none o' thievin' Berry Hamilton's fambly to speak to me."

"Why, you were all right this evening."

"Yes, but jest out o' pity, an' you was nice 'cause you was afraid I'd tell on you. Go on now."

"Go on now," said Minty's young man; and he looked menacing.

Joe, what little self-respect he had gone, slunk out of the room and needed several whiskeys in a neighbouring saloon to give him courage to go to the theatre and wait for Hattie, who was playing in vaudeville houses pending the opening of her company.

The closing act was just over when he reached the stage door. He was there but a short time, when Hattie tripped out and took his arm. Her face was bright and smiling, and there was no suggestion of disgust in the dancing eyes she turned up to him. Evidently she had not heard, but the thought gave him no particular pleasure, as it left him in suspense as to how she would act when she should hear.

"Let's go somewhere and get some supper," she said; "I'm as hungry as I can be. What are you looking so cut up about?"

"Oh, I ain't feelin' so very good."

"I hope you ain't lettin' that long-tongued Brown woman bother your head, are you?"

His heart seemed to stand still. She did know, then.

"Do you know all about it?"

"Why, of course I do. You might know she'd come to me first with her story."

"And you still keep on speaking to me?"

"Now look here, Joe, if you've been drinking, I'll forgive you; if you ain't, you go on and leave me. Say, what do you take me for? Do you think I'd throw down a friend because somebody else talked about him? Well, you don't know Hat Sterling. When Minty told me that story, she was back in my dressing-room, and I sent her out o' there a-flying, and with a tongue-lashing that she won't forget for a month o' Sundays."

"I reckon that was the reason she jumped on me so hard at the club." He chuckled. He had taken heart again. All that Sadness had said was true, after all, and people thought no less of him. His joy was unbounded.

"So she jumped on you hard, did she? The cat!"

"Oh, she didn't say a thing to me."

"Well, Joe, it's just like this. I ain't an angel—you know that—but I do try to be square, and whenever I find a friend of mine down on his luck, in his pocket-book or his feelings, why, I give him my flipper. Why, old chap, I believe I like you better for the stiff upper lip you've been keeping under all this."

"Why, Hattie," he broke out, unable any longer to control himself, "you're—you're—"

"Oh, I'm just plain Hat Sterling, who won't throw down her friends. Now come on and get something to eat. If that thing is at the club, we'll go there and show her just how much her talk amounted to. She thinks she's the whole game, but I can spot her and then show her that she ain't one, two, three."

When they reached the Banner, they found Minty still there. She tried on the two the same tactics that she had employed so successfully upon Joe alone. She nudged her companion and tittered. But she had another person to deal with. Hattie Sterling stared at her coldly and in-differently, and passed on by her to a seat. Joe proceeded to order supper and other things in the nonchalant way that the woman had enjoined upon him. Minty began to feel distinctly uncomfortable, but it was her business not to be beaten. She laughed outright. Hattie did not seem to hear her. She was beckoning Sadness to her side. He came and sat down.

"Now look here," she said, "you can't have any supper because you haven't reached the stage of magnificent hunger to make a meal palatable to you. You've got so used to being nearly starved that a meal don't taste good to you under any other circumstances. You're in on the drinks, though. Your thirst is always available.—Jack," she called down the long room to the bartender, "make it three.—Lean over here. I want to talk to you. See that woman over there by the wall? No, not that one,—the big light woman with Griggs. Well, she's come here with a story trying to throw Joe down, and I want you to help me do her."

"Oh, that's the one that upset our young friend, is it?" said Sadness, turning his mournful eyes upon Minty.

"That's her. So you know about it, do you?"

"Yes, and I'll help do her. She mustn't touch one of the fraternity, you know." He kept his eyes fixed upon the outsider until she squirmed. She could not at all understand this serious conversation directed at her. She wondered if she had gone too far and if they contemplated putting her out. It made her uneasy.

Now, this same Miss Sterling had the faculty of attracting a good deal of attention when she wished to. She brought it into play to-night, and in ten minutes, aided by Sadness, she had a crowd of jolly people about her table. When, as she would have expressed it, "everything was going fat," she suddenly paused and, turning her eyes full upon Minty, said in a voice loud enough for all to hear,—

"Say, boys, you've heard that story about Joe, haven't you?"

They had.

"Well, that's the one that told it; she's come here to try to throw him and me down. Is she going to do it?"

"Well, I guess not!" was the rousing reply, and every face turned towards the now frightened Minty. She rose hastily and, getting her skirts together, fled from the room, followed more leisurely by the crestfallen Griggs. Hattie's laugh and "Thank you, fellows," followed her out.

Matters were less easy for Joe's mother and sister than they were for him. A week or more after this, Kitty found him and told him that Minty's story had reached their employers and that they were out of work.

"You see, Joe," she said sadly, "we've took a flat since we moved from Mis' Jones', and we had to furnish it. We've got one lodger, a race-horse man, an' he's mighty nice to ma an' me, but that ain't enough. Now we've got to do something."

Joe was so smitten with sorrow that he gave her a dollar and promised to speak about the matter to a friend of his.

He did speak about it to Hattie.

"You've told me once or twice that your sister could sing. Bring her down here to me, and if she can do anything, I'll get her a place on the stage," was Hattie's answer.

When Kitty heard it she was radiant, but her mother only shook her head and said, "De las' hope, de las' hope."

CHAPTER 12

"All the World's a Stage"

KITTY PROVED HERSELF Joe's sister by falling desperately
in love with Hattie Sterling the first time they met. The
actress was very gracious to her, and called her "child"
in a pretty, patronizing way, and patted her on the
cheek.

"It's a shame that Joe hasn't brought you around before. We've been good friends for quite some time."

"He told me you an' him was right good friends."

Already Joe took on a new importance in his sister's
eyes. He must be quite a man, she thought, to be the
friend of such a person as Miss Sterling.

"So you think you want to go on the stage, do you?"

"Yes, 'm, I thought it might be right nice for me if I
could."

"Joe, go out and get some beer for us, and then I'll
hear your sister sing."

Miss Sterling talked as if she were a manager and
had only to snap her fingers to be obeyed. When Joe
came back with the beer, Kitty drank a glass. She did not
like it, but she would not offend her hostess. After this
she sang, and Miss Sterling applauded her generously,
although the young girl's nervousness kept her from

doing her best. The encouragement helped her, and she did better as she became more at home.

"Why, child, you've got a good voice. And, Joe, you've been keeping her shut up all this time. You ought to be ashamed of yourself."

The young man had little to say. He had brought Kitty almost under a protest, because he had no confidence in her ability and thought that his "girl" would disillusion her. It did not please him now to find his sister so fully under the limelight and himself "up stage."

Kitty was quite in a flutter of delight—not so much with the idea of working as with the glamour of the work she might be allowed to do.

"I tell you, now," Hattie Sterling pursued, throwing a brightly stockinged foot upon a chair, "your voice is too good for the chorus. Gi' me a cigarette, Joe. Have one, Kitty?—I'm goin' to call you Kitty. It's nice and home-like, and then we've got to be great chums, you know."

Kitty, unwilling to refuse anything from the sorceress, took her cigarette and lighted it, but a few puffs set her off coughing.

"Tut, tut, Kitty, child, don't do it if you ain't used to it. You'll learn soon enough."

Joe wanted to kick his sister for having tried so delicate an art and failed, for he had not yet lost all of his awe of Hattie.

"Now, what I was going to say," the lady resumed after several contemplative puffs, "is that you'll have to begin in the chorus any way and work your way up. It wouldn't take long for you, with your looks and voice, to put one of the 'up and ups' out o' the business. Only hope it won't be me. I've had people I've helped try to do it often enough."

She gave a laugh that had just a touch of bitterness

in it, for she began to recognize that although she had been on the stage only a short time, she was no longer the all-conquering Hattie Sterling, in the first freshness of her youth.

"Oh, I wouldn't want to push anybody out," Kit expostulated.

"Oh, never mind, you'll soon get bravely over that feeling, and even if you didn't it wouldn't matter much. The thing has to happen. Somebody's got to go down. We don't last long in this life: it soon wears us out, and when we're worn out and sung out, danced out and played out, the manager has no further use for us; so he reduces us to the ranks or kicks us out entirely."

Joe here thought it time for him to put in a word. "Get out, Hat," he said contemptuously; "you're good for a dozen years yet."

She didn't deign to notice him, save so far as a sniff goes.

"Don't you let what I say scare you, though, Kitty. You've got a good chance, and maybe you'll have more sense than I've got, and at least save money—while you're in it. But let's get off that. It makes me sick. All you've got to do is to come to the opera-house to-morrow and I'll introduce you to the manager. He's a fool, but I think we can make him do something for you."

"Oh, thank you, I'll be around to-morrow, sure."

"Better come about ten o'clock. There's a rehearsal to-morrow, and you'll find him there. Of course, he'll be pretty rough, he always is at rehearsals, but he'll take to you if he thinks there's anything in you and he can get it out."

Kitty felt herself dismissed and rose to go. Joe did not rise.

"I'll see you later, Kit," he said; "I ain't goin' just yet.

Say," he added, when his sister was gone, "you're a hot one. What do you want to give her all that con for? She'll never get in."

"Joe," said Hattie, "don't you get awful tired of being a jackass? Sometimes I want to kiss you, and sometimes I feel as if I had to kick you. I'll compromise with you now by letting you bring me some more beer. This got all stale while your sister was here. I saw she didn't like it, and so I wouldn't drink any more for fear she'd try to keep up with me."

"Kit is a good deal of a jay yet," Joe remarked wisely.

"Oh, yes, this world is full of jays. Lots of 'em have seen enough to make 'em wise, but they're still jays, and don't know it. That's the worst of it. They go around thinking they're it, when they ain't even in the game. Go on and get the beer."

And Joe went, feeling vaguely that he had been sat upon.

Kit flew home with joyous heart to tell her mother of her good prospects. She had burst into the room, crying, "Oh, ma, ma, Miss Hattie thinks I'll do to go on the stage. Ain't it grand?"

She did not meet with the expected warmth of response from her mother.

"I do' know as it'll be so gran'. F'om what I see of dem stage people dey don't seem to 'mount to much. De way dem gals shows demse'ves is right down bad to me. Is you goin' to dress lak dem we seen dat night?"

Kit hung her head.

"I guess I'll have to."

"Well, ef you have to, I'd ruther see you daid any day. Oh, Kit, my little gal, don't do it, don't do it. Don't you go down lak yo' brothah Joe. Joe's gone."

"Why, ma, you don't understand. Joe's somebody now.

You ought to 've heard how Miss Hattie talked about him. She said he's been her friend for a long while."

"Her frien', yes, an' his own inimy. You needn' pattern aftah dat gal, Kit. She ruint Joe, an' she's aftah you now."

"But nowadays everybody thinks stage people respectable up here."

"Maybe I'm ol'-fashioned, but I can't believe in any ooman's ladyship when she shows herse'f lak dem gals does. Oh, Kit, don't do it. Ain't you seen enough? Don't you know enough already to stay away fom dese hyeah people? Dey don't want nothin' but to pull you down an' den laugh at you w'en you's dragged in de dust."

"You mustn't feel that away, ma. I'm doin' it to help you."

"I do' want no sich help. I'd ruther starve."

Kit did not reply, but there was no yielding in her manner.

"Kit," her mother went on, "dey's somep'n I ain't nevah tol' you dat I'm goin' to tell you now. Mistah Gibson ust to come to Mis' Jones's lots to see me befo' we moved hyeah, an' he's been talkin' 'bout a good many things to me." She hesitated. "He say dat I ain't noways ma'ied to my po' husban', dat a pen'tentiary sentence is de same as a divo'ce, an' if Be'y should live to git out, we'd have to ma'y ag'in. I wouldn't min' dat, Kit, but he say dat at Be'y's age dey ain't much chanst of his livin' to git out, an' hyeah I'll live all dis time alone, an' den have no one to tek keer o' me w'en I git ol'. He wants me to ma'y him, Kit. Kit, I love yo' fathah; he's my only one. But Joe, he's gone, an' ef yo go, befo' Gawd I'll tell Tawm Gibson yes."

The mother looked up to see just what effect her plea would have on her daughter. She hoped that what she said would have the desired result. But the girl turned around from fixing her neck-ribbon before the glass, her face radiant. "Why, it'll be splendid. He's such a nice man, an' race-horse men 'most always have money. Why don't you marry him, ma? Then I'd feel that you was safe an' settled, an' that you wouldn't be lonesome when the show was out of town."

"You want me to ma'y him an' desert yo' po' pa?"

"I guess what he says is right, ma. I don't reckon we'll ever see pa again an' you got to do something. You got to live for yourself now."

Her mother dropped her head in her hands. "All right," she said, "I'll do it; I'll ma'y him. I might as well go de way both my chillen's gone. Po' Be'y, po' Be'y. Ef you evah do come out, Gawd he'p you to baih what you'll fin'." And Mrs. Hamilton rose and tottered from the room, as if the old age she anticipated had already come upon her.

Kit stood looking after her, fear and grief in her eyes. "Poor ma," she said, "an' poor pa. But I know, an' I know it's for the best."

On the next morning she was up early and practising hard for her interview with the managing star of "Martin's Blackbirds."

When she arrived at the theatre, Hattie Sterling met her with frank friendliness.

"I'm glad you came early, Kitty," she remarked, "for maybe you can get a chance to talk with Martin before he begins rehearsal and gets all worked up. He'll be a little less like a bear then. But even if you don't see him before then, wait, and don't get scared if he tries to bluff you. His bark is a good deal worse than his bite."

When Mr. Martin came in that morning, he had other ideas than that of seeing applicants for places. His show must begin in two weeks, and it was advertised to be larger and better than ever before, when really nothing at all had been done for it. The promise of this advertisement must be fulfilled. Mr. Martin was late, and was out of humour with every one else on account of it. He came in hurried, fierce, and important.

"Mornin', Mr. Smith, mornin', Mrs. Jones. Ha, ladies and gentlemen, all here?"

He shot every word out of his mouth as if the aftertaste of it were unpleasant to him. He walked among the chorus like an angry king among his vassals, and his glance was a flash of insolent fire. From his head to his feet he was the very epitome of self-sufficient, brutal conceit.

Kitty trembled as she noted the hush that fell on the people at his entrance. She felt like rushing out of the room. She could never face this terrible man. She trembled more as she found his eyes fixed upon her.

"Who's that?" he asked, disregarding her, as if she had been a stick or a stone.

"Well, don't snap her head off. It's a girl friend of mine that wants a place," said Hattie. She was the only one who would brave Martin.

"Humph. Let her wait. I ain't got no time to hear any one now. Get yourselves in line, you all who are on to that first chorus, while I'm getting into my sweat-shirt."

He disappeared behind a screen, whence he emerged arrayed, or only half arrayed, in a thick absorbing shirt and a thin pair of woolen trousers. Then the work began. The man was indefatigable. He was like the spirit of energy. He was in every place about the stage at once, leading the chorus, showing them steps, twisting some awkward girl into shape, shouting, gesticulating, abusing the pianist.

"Now, now," he would shout, "the left foot on that

beat. Bah, bah, stop! You walk like a lot of tin soldiers. Are your joints rusty? Do you want oil? Look here, Taylor, if I didn't know you, I'd take you for a truck. Pick up your feet, open your mouths, and move, move, move! Oh!" and he would drop his head in despair. "And to think that I've got to do something with these things in two weeks—two weeks!" Then he would turn to them again with a sudden reaccession of eagerness. "Now, at it again, at it again! Hold that note, hold it! Now whirl, and on the left foot. Stop that music, stop it! Miss Coster, you'll learn that step in about a thousand years, and I've got nine hundred and ninety-nine years and fifty weeks less time than that to spare. Come here and try that step with me. Don't be afraid to move. Step like a chicken on a hot griddle!" And some blushing girl would come forward and go through the step alone before all the rest.

Kitty contemplated the scene with a mind equally divided between fear and anger. What should she do if he should so speak to her? Like the others, no doubt, smile sheepishly and obey him. But she did not like to believe it. She felt that the independence which she had known from babyhood would assert itself, and that she would talk back to him, even as Hattie Sterling did. She felt scared and discouraged, but every now and then her friend smiled encouragingly upon her across the ranks of moving singers.

Finally, however, her thoughts were broken in upon by hearing Mr. Martin cry: "Oh, quit, quit, and go rest yourselves, you ancient pieces of hickory, and let me forget you for a minute before I go crazy. Where's that new girl now?"

Kitty rose and went toward him, trembling so that she could hardly walk.

"What can you do?"

"I can sing," very faintly.

"Well, if that's the voice you're going to sing in, there won't be many that'll know whether it's good or bad. Well, let's hear something. Do you know any of these?"

And he ran over the titles of several songs. She knew some of them, and he selected one. "Try this. Here, Tom, play it for her."

It was an ordeal for the girl to go through. She had never sung before at anything more formidable than a church concert, where only her immediate acquaintances and townspeople were present. Now to sing before all these strange people, themselves singers, made her feel faint and awkward. But the courage of desperation came to her, and she struck into the song. At the first her voice wavered and threatened to fail her. It must not. She choked back her fright and forced the music from her lips.

When she was done, she was startled to hear Martin burst into a raucous laugh. Such humiliation! She had failed, and instead of telling her, he was bringing her to shame before the whole company. The tears came into her eyes, and she was about giving way when she caught a reassuring nod and smile from Hattie Sterling, and seized on this as a last hope.

"Haw, haw, haw!" laughed Martin, "haw, haw haw! The little one was scared, see? She was scared, d' you understand? But did you see the grit she went at it with? Just took the bit in her teeth and got away. Haw, haw, haw! Now, that's what I like. If all you girls had that spirit, we could do something in two weeks. Try another one, girl."

Kitty's heart had suddenly grown light. She sang the second one better because something within her was singing.

"Good!" said Martin, but he immediately returned to

his cold manner. "You watch these girls close and see what they do, and to-morrow be prepared to go into line and move as well as sing."

He immediately turned his attention from her to the chorus, but no slight that he could inflict upon her now could take away the sweet truth that she was engaged and to-morrow would begin work. She wished she could go over and embrace Hattie Sterling. She thought kindly of Joe, and promised herself to give him a present out of her first month's earnings.

On the first night of the show pretty little Kitty Hamilton was pointed out as a girl who wouldn't be in the chorus long. The mother, who was soon to be Mrs. Gibson, sat in the balcony, a grieved, pained look on her face. Joe was in a front row with some of the rest of his gang. He took many drinks between the acts, because he was proud.

Mr. Thomas was there. He also was proud, and after the performance he waited for Kitty at the stage door and went forward to meet her as she came out. The look she gave him stopped him, and he let her pass without a word.

"Who'd 'a' thought," he mused, "that the kid had that much nerve? Well, if they don't want to find out things, what do they come to N' Yawk for? It ain't nobody's old Sunday-school picnic. Guess I got out easy, anyhow."

Hattie Sterling took Joe home in a hansom.

"Say," she said, "if you come this way for me again, it's all over, see? Your little sister's a comer, and I've got to hustle to keep up with her."

Joe growled and fell asleep in his chair. One must needs have a strong head or a strong will when one is the brother of a celebrity and would celebrate the distinguished one's success.

CHAPTER 13

The Oakleys

A YEAR AFTER the arrest of Berry Hamilton, and at a time when New York had shown to the eyes of his family so many strange new sights, there were few changes to be noted in the condition of affairs at the Oakley place. Maurice Oakley was perhaps a shade more distrustful of his servants, and consequently more testy with them. Mrs. Oakley was the same acquiescent woman, with unbounded faith in her husband's wisdom and judgment. With complacent minds both went their ways, drank their wine, and said their prayers, and wished that brother Frank's five years were past. They had letters from him now and then, never very cheerful in tone, but always breathing the deepest love and gratitude to them.

His brother found deep cause for congratulation in the tone of these epistles.

"Frank is getting down to work," he would cry exultantly. "He is past the first buoyant enthusiasm of youth. Ah, Leslie, when a man begins to be serious, then he begins to be something." And her only answer would be, "I wonder, Maurice, if Claire Lessing will wait for him."

The two had frequent questions to answer as to Frank's doing and prospects, and they had always bright things to say of him, even when his letters gave them no such warrant. Their love for him made them read large between the lines, and all they read was good.

Between Maurice and his brother no word of the guilty servant ever passed. They each avoided it as an unpleasant subject. Frank had never asked and his brother had never proffered aught of the outcome of the case.

Mrs. Oakley had once suggested it. "Brother ought to know," she said, "that Berry is being properly punished."

"By no means," replied her husband. "You know that it would only hurt him. He shall never know if I have to tell him."

"You are right, Maurice—you are always right. We must shield Frank from the pain it would cause him. Poor fellow! he is so sensitive."

Their hearts were still steadfastly fixed upon the union of this younger brother with Claire Lessing. She had lately come into a fortune, and there was nothing now to prevent it. They would have written Frank to urge it, but they both believed that to try to woo him away from his art was but to make him more wayward. That any woman could have power enough to take him away from this jealous mistress they very much doubted. But they could hope, and hope made them eager to open every letter that bore the French postmark. Always it might contain news that he was coming home, or that he had made a great success, or, better, some inquiry after Claire. A long time they had waited, but found no such tidings in the letters from Paris.

At last, as Maurice Oakley sat in his library one day, the servant brought him a letter more bulky in weight and appearance than any he had yet received. His eyes glistened with pleasure as he read the postmark. "A letter from Frank," he said joyfully, "and an important one, I'll wager."

He smiled as he weighed it in his hand and caressed it. Mrs. Oakley was out shopping, and as he knew how deep her interest was, he hesitated to break the seal before she returned. He curbed his natural desire and laid the heavy envelope down on the desk. But he could not deny himself the pleasure of speculating as to its contents.

It was such a large, interesting-looking package. What might it contain? It simply reeked of possibilities. Had any one banteringly told Maurice Oakley that he had such a deep vein of sentiment, he would have denied it with scorn and laughter. But here he found himself sitting with the letter in his hand and weaving stories as to its contents.

First, now, it might be a notice that Frank had received the badge of the Legion of Honour. No, no, that was too big, and he laughed aloud at his own folly, wondering the next minute, with half shame, why he laughed, for did he, after all, believe anything was too big for that brother of his? Well, let him begin, anyway, away down. Let him say, for instance, that the letter told of the completion and sale of a great picture. Frank had sold small ones. He would be glad of this, for his brother had written him several times of things that were a-doing, but not yet of anything that was done. Or, better yet, let the letter say that some picture, long finished, but of which the artist's pride and anxiety had forbidden him to speak, had made a glowing success, the success it deserved. This sounded well, and seemed not at all beyond the bounds of possibility. It was an alluring vision. He saw the picture already. It was a scene from life, true in detail to the point of very minuteness, and yet with something spiritual in it that lifted it above the mere copy of the commonplace. At the Salon it would be hung on the line, and people would stand before it, admiring its workmanship and asking who the artist was. He drew on his memory of old reading. In his mind's eye he saw Frank, unconscious of his own power or too modest to admit it, stand unknown among the crowds around his picture waiting for and dreading their criticisms. He saw the light leap to his eyes as he heard their words of praise. He saw the straightening of his narrow shoulders when he was forced to admit that he was the painter of the work. Then the windows of Paris were filled with his portraits. The papers were full of his praise, and brave men and fair women met together to do him homage. Fair women, yes, and Frank would look upon them all and see reflected in them but a tithe of the glory of one woman, and that woman Claire Lessing. He roused himself and laughed again as he tapped the magic envelope.

"My fancies go on and conquer the world for my brother," he muttered. "He will follow their flight one day and do it himself."

The letter drew his eyes back to it. It seemed to invite him, to beg him even. "No, I will not do it; I will wait until Leslie comes. She will be as glad to hear the good news as I am."

His dreams were taking the shape of reality in his mind, and he was believing all that he wanted to believe.

He turned to look at a picture painted by Frank which hung over the mantel. He dwelt lovingly upon it, seeing in it the touch of a genius.

"Surely," he said, "this new picture cannot be greater than that, though it shall hang where kings can see it and this only graces the library of my poor house. It has the feeling of a woman's soul with the strength of a man's heart. When Frank and Claire marry, I shall give it back to them. It is too great a treasure for a clod like me. Heigho, why will women be so long a-shopping?"

He glanced again at the letter, and his hand went out involuntarily towards it. He fondled it, smiling.

"Ah, Lady Leslie, I've a mind to open it to punish you for staying so long."

He essayed to be playful, but he knew that he was trying to make a compromise with himself because his eagerness grew stronger than his gallantry. He laid the letter down and picked it up again. He studied the postmark over and over. He got up and walked to the window and back again, and then began fumbling in his pockets for his knife. No, he did not want it; yes, he did. He would just cut the envelope and make believe he had read it to pique his wife; but he would not read it. Yes, that was it. He found the knife and slit the paper. His fingers trembled as he touched the sheets that protruded. Why would not Leslie come? Did she not know that he was waiting for her? She ought to have known that there was a letter from Paris to-day, for it had been a month since they had had one.

There was a sound of footsteps without. He sprang up, crying, "I've been waiting so long for you!" A servant opened the door to bring him a message. Oakley dismissed him angrily. What did he want to go down to the Continental for to drink and talk politics to a lot of muddle-pated fools when he had a brother in Paris who was an artist and a letter from him lay unread in his hand? His patience and his temper were going. Leslie was careless and unfeeling. She ought to come; he was tired of waiting.

A carriage rolled up the driveway and he dropped the letter guiltily, as if it were not his own. He would only say that he had grown tired of waiting and started to read it. But it was only Mrs. Davis's footman leaving a note for Leslie about some charity.

He went back to the letter. Well, it was his. Leslie had forfeited her right to see it as soon as he. It might be mean, but it was not dishonest. No, he would not read it now, but he would take it and show her that he had exercised his self-control in spite of her shortcomings. He laid it on the desk once more. It leered at him. He might just open the sheets enough to see the lines that began it, and read no further. Yes, he would do that. Leslie could not feel hurt at such a little thing.

The first line had only "Dear Brother." "Dear Brother"! Why not the second? That could not hold much more. The second line held him, and the third, and the fourth, and as he read on, unmindful now of what Leslie might think or feel, his face turned from the ruddy glow of pleasant anxiety to the pallor of grief and terror. He was not half-way through it when Mrs. Oakley's voice in the hall announced her coming. He did not hear her. He sat staring at the page before him, his lips apart and his eyes staring. Then, with a cry that echoed through the house, crumpling the sheets in his hand, he fell forward, fainting to the floor, just as his wife rushed into the room.

"What is it?" she cried. "Maurice! Maurice!"

He lay on the floor, staring up at the ceiling, the letter clutched in his hands. She ran to him and lifted up his head, but he gave no sign of life. Already the servants were crowding to the door. She bade one of them to hasten for a doctor, others to bring water and brandy, and the rest to be gone. As soon as she was alone, she loosed the crumpled sheets from his hand, for she felt that this must have been the cause of her husband's strange attack. Without a thought of wrong, for they had no secrets from each other, she glanced at the opening lines. Then she forgot the unconscious man at her feet and read the letter through to the end.

The letter was in Frank's neat hand, a little shaken, perhaps, by nervousness.

"DEAR BROTHER," it ran, "I know you will grieve at receiving this, and I wish that I might bear your grief for you, but I cannot, though I have as heavy a burden as this can bring to you. Mine would have been lighter to-day, perhaps, had you been more straightforward with me. I am not blaming you, however, for I know that my hypocrisy made you believe me possessed of a really soft heart, and you thought to spare me. Until yesterday, when in a letter from Esterton he casually mentioned the matter, I did not know that Berry was in prison, else this letter would have been written sooner. I have been wanting to write it for so long, and yet have been too great a coward to do so.

"I know that you will be disappointed in me, and just what that disappointment will cost you I know; but you must hear the truth. I shall never see your face again, or I should not dare to tell it even now. You will remember that I begged you to be easy on your servant. You thought it was only my kindness of heart. It was not; I had a deeper reason. I knew where the money had gone and dared not tell. Berry is as innocent as yourself— and I—well, it is a story, and let me tell it to you.

"You have had so much confidence in me, and I hate to tell you that it was all misplaced. I have no doubt that I should not be doing it now but that I have drunken absinthe enough to give me the emotional point of view, which I shall regret to-morrow. I do not mean that I am drunk. I can think clearly and write clearly, but my emotions are extremely active.

"Do you remember Claire's saying at the table that night of the farewell dinner that some dark-eyed mademoiselle was waiting for me? She did not know how truly she spoke, though I fancy she saw how I flushed when she said it: for I was already in love—madly so.

"I need not describe her. I need say nothing about her, for I know that nothing I say can ever persuade you to forgive her for taking me from you. This has gone on since I first came here, and I dared not tell you, for I saw whither your eyes had turned. I loved this girl, and she both inspired and hindered my work. Perhaps I would have been successful had I not met her, perhaps not.

"I love her too well to marry her and make of our devotion a stale, prosy thing of duty and compulsion. When a man does not marry a woman, he must keep her better than he would a wife. It costs. All that you gave me went to make her happy.

"Then, when I was about leaving you, the catastrophe came. I wanted much to carry back to her. I gambled to make more. I would surprise her. Luck was against me. Night after night I lost. Then, just before the dinner, I woke from my frenzy to find all that I had was gone. I would have asked you for more, and you would have given it; but that strange, ridiculous something which we misname Southern honour, that honour which strains at a gnat and swallows a camel, withheld me, and I preferred to do worse. So I lied to you. The money

from my cabinet was not stolen save by myself. I
am a liar and a thief, but your eyes shall never tell
me so.

"Tell the truth and have Berry released. I can
stand it. Write me but one letter to tell me of this.
Do not plead with me, do not forgive me, do not
seek to find me, for from this time I shall be as
one who has perished from the earth; I shall be
no more.

"Your brother,

"FRANK."

By the time the servants came they found Mrs. Oakley
as white as her lord. But with firm hands and compressed
lips she ministered to his needs pending the doctor's ar-
rival. She bathed his face and temples, chafed his hands,
and forced the brandy between his lips. Finally he stirred
and his hands gripped.

"The letter!" he gasped.

"Yes, dear. I have it; I have it."

"Give it to me," he cried. She handed it to him. He
seized it and thrust it into his breast.

"Did—did—you read it?"

"Yes, I did not know—"

"Oh, my God, I did not intend that you should see it. I
wanted the secret for my own. I wanted to carry it to my
grave with me. Oh, Frank, Frank, Frank!"

"Never mind, Maurice. It is as if you alone knew it."

"It is not, I say, it is not!"

He turned upon his face and began to weep passion-
ately, not like a man, but like a child whose last toy has
been broken.

"Oh, my God," he moaned, "my brother, my brother!"

"'Sh, dearie, think—it's—it's—Frank."

"That's it, that's it—that's what I can't forget. It's Frank,—Frank, my brother."

Suddenly he sat up and his eyes stared straight into hers.

"Leslie, no one must ever know what is in this letter," he said calmly.

"No one shall, Maurice; come, let us burn it."

"Burn it? No, no," he cried, clutching at his breast. "It must not be burned. What! burn my brother's secret? No, no, I must carry it with me,—carry it with me to the grave."

"But, Maurice——"

"I must carry it with me."

She saw that he was overwrought, and so did not argue with him.

When the doctor came, he found Maurice Oakley in bed, but better. The medical man diagnosed the case and decided that he had received some severe shock. He feared too for his heart, for the patient constantly held his hands pressed against his bosom. In vain the doctor pleaded; he would not take them down, and when the wife added her word, the physician gave up and, after prescribing, left, much puzzled in mind.

"It's a strange case," he said; "there's something more than the nervous shock that makes him clutch his chest like that, and yet I have never noticed signs of heart trouble in Oakley. Oh, well, business worry will produce anything in anybody."

It was soon common talk about the town about Maurice Oakley's attack. In the seclusion of his chamber he was saying to his wife:

"Ah, Leslie, you and I will keep the secret. No one shall ever know."

"Yes, dear, but—but—what of Berry?"

"What of Berry?" he cried, starting up excitedly. "What is Berry to Frank? What is that nigger to my brother? What are his sufferings to the honor of my family and name?"

"Never mind, Maurice, never mind. You are right."

"It must never be known, I say, if Berry has to rot in jail."

So they wrote a lie to Frank, and buried the secret in their breasts, and Oakley wore its visible form upon his heart.

CHAPTER 14

Frankenstein

FIVE YEARS IS but a short time in the life of a man, and yet many things may happen therein. For instance, the whole way of a family's life may be changed. Good natures may be made into bad ones and out of a soul of faith grow a spirit of unbelief. The independence of respectability may harden into the insolence of defiance, and the sensitive cheek of modesty into the brazen face of shamelessness. It may be true that the habits of years are hard to change, but this is not true of the first sixteen or seventeen years of a young person's life, else Kitty Hamilton and Joe could not so easily have become what they were. It had taken barely five years to accomplish an entire metamorphosis of their characters. In Joe's case even a shorter time was needed. He was so ready to go down that it needed but a gentle push to start him, and once started, there was nothing within him to hold him back from the depths. For his will was as flabby as his conscience, and his pride, which stands to some men for conscience, had no definite aim or direction.

Hattie Sterling had given him both his greatest impulse for evil and for good. She had at first given him his gentle push, but when she saw that his collapse would lose her a faithful and useful slave she had sought to check his course. Her threat of the severance of their relations had held him up for a little time, and she began to believe that he was safe again. He went back to the work he had neglected, drank moderately, and acted in most things as a sound, sensible being. Then, all of a sudden, he went down again, and went down badly. She kept her promise and threw him over. Then he became a hanger-on at the clubs, a genteel loafer. He used to say in his sober moments that at last he was one of the boys that Sadness had spoken of. He did not work, and yet he lived and ate and was proud of his degradation But he soon tired of being separated from Hattie, and straightened up again. After some demur she received him upon his former footing. It was only for a few months. He fell again. For almost four years this had happened intermittently. Finally he took a turn for the better that endured so long that Hattie Sterling gave him her faith. Then the woman made her mistake. She warmed to him. She showed him that she was proud of him. He went forth at once to celebrate his victory. He did not return to her for three days. Then he was battered, unkempt, and thick of speech.

She looked at him in silent contempt for a while as he sat nursing his aching head.

"Well, you're a beauty," she said finally with cutting scorn. "You ought to be put under a glass case and placed on exhibition."

He groaned and his head sunk lower. A drunken man is always disarmed.

His helplessness, instead of inspiring her with pity, inflamed her with an unfeeling anger that burst forth in a volume of taunts.

"You're the thing I've given up all my chances for—you, a miserable, drunken jay, without a jay's decency.

No one had ever looked at you until I picked you up and you've been strutting around ever since, showing off because I was kind to you, and now this is the way you pay me back. Drunk half the time and half drunk the rest. Well, you know what I told you the last time you got 'loaded'? I mean it too. You're not the only star in sight, see?"

She laughed meanly and began to sing, "You'll have to find another baby now."

For the first time he looked up, and his eyes were full of tears—tears both of grief and intoxication. There was an expression of a whipped dog on his face.

"Do'—Ha'ie, do'—" he pleaded, stretching out his hands to her.

Her eyes blazed back at him, but she sang on insolently, tauntingly.

The very inanity of the man disgusted her, and on a sudden impulse she sprang up and struck him full in the face with the flat of her hand. He was too weak to resist the blow, and, tumbling from the chair, fell limply to the floor, where he lay at her feet, alternately weeping aloud and quivering with drunken, hiccoughing sobs.

"Get up!" she cried; "get up and get out o' here. You sha'n't lay around my house."

He had already begun to fall into a drunken sleep, but she shook him, got him to his feet, and pushed him outside the door. "Now, go, you drunken dog, and never put your foot inside this house again."

He stood outside, swaying dizzily upon his feet and looking back with dazed eyes at the door; then he muttered: "Pu' me out, wi' you? Pu' me out, damn you! Well, I ki' you. See 'f I don't;" and he half walked, half fell down the street.

Sadness and Skaggsy were together at the club that

night. Five years had not changed the latter as to wealth or position or inclination, and he was still a frequent visitor at the Banner. He always came in alone now, for Maudie had gone the way of all the half-world, and reached depths to which Mr. Skaggs's job prevented him from following her. However, he mourned truly for his lost companion, and to-night he was in a particularly pensive mood.

Some one was playing rag-time on the piano, and the dancers were wheeling in time to the music. Skaggsy looked at them regretfully as he sipped his liquor. It made him think of Maudie. He sighed and turned away.

"I tell you, Sadness," he said impulsively, "dancing is the poetry of motion."

"Yes," replied Sadness, "and dancing in rag-time is the dialect poetry."

The reporter did not like this. It savoured of flippancy, and he was about entering upon a discussion to prove that Sadness had no soul, when Joe, with bloodshot eyes and dishevelled clothes, staggered in and reeled towards them.

"Drunk again," said Sadness. "Really, it's a waste of time for Joe to sober up. Hullo there!" as the young man brought up against him; "take a seat." He put him in a chair at the table. "Been lushin' a bit, eh?"

"Gi' me some'n' drink."

"Oh, a hair of the dog. Some men shave their dogs clean, and then have hydrophobia. Here, Jack!"

They drank, and then, as if the whiskey had done him good, Joe sat up in his chair.

"Ha'ie's throwed me down."

"Lucky dog! You might have known it would have happened sooner or later. Better sooner than never."

Skaggs smoked in silence and looked at Joe.

"I'm goin' to kill her."

"I wouldn't if I were you. Take old Sadness's advice and thank your stars that you're rid of her."

"I'm goin' to kill her." He paused and looked at them drowsily. Then, bracing himself up again, he broke out suddenly, "Say, d' ever tell y' 'bout the ol' man? He never stole that money. Know he di' n'."

He threatened to fall asleep now, but the reporter was all alert. He scented a story.

"By Jove!" he exclaimed, "did you hear that? Bet the chap stole it himself and's letting the old man suffer for it. Great story, ain't it? Come, come, wake up here. Three more, Jack. What about your father?"

"Father? Who's father. Oh, do' bother me. What?"

"Here, here, tell us about your father and the money. If he didn't steal it, who did?"

"Who did? Tha' 's it. Who did? Ol' man di' n' steal it, know he di' n'."

"Oh, let him alone, Skaggsy. He don't know what he's saying."

"Yes, he does. A drunken man tells the truth."

"In some cases," said Sadness.

"Oh, let me alone, man. I've been trying for years to get a big sensation for my paper, and if this story is one, I'm a made man."

The drink seemed to revive the young man again, and by bits Skaggs was able to pick out of him the story of his father's arrest and conviction. At its close he relapsed into stupidity, murmuring, "She throwed me down."

"Well," sneered Sadness, "you see drunken men tell the truth, and you don't seem to get much guilt out of our young friend. You're disappointed, aren't you?"

"I confess I am disappointed, but I've got an idea, just the same."

"Oh, you have? Well, don't handle it carelessly; it might go off." And Sadness rose. The reporter sat thinking for a time and then followed him, leaving Joe in a drunken sleep at the table. There he lay for more than two hours. When he finally awoke, he started up as if some determination had come to him in his sleep. A part of the helplessness of his intoxication had gone, but his first act was to call for more whiskey. This he gulped down, and followed with another and another. For a while he stood still, brooding silently, his red eyes blinking at the light. Then he turned abruptly and left the club.

It was very late when he reached Hattie's door, but he opened it with his latch-key, as he had been used to do. He stopped to help himself to a glass of brandy, as he had so often done before. Then he went directly to her room. She was a light sleeper, and his step awakened her.

"Who is it?" she cried in affright.

"It's me." His voice was steadier now, but grim.

"What do you want? Didn't I tell you never to come here again? Get out or I'll have you taken out."

She sprang up in bed, glaring angrily at him.

His hands twitched nervously, as if her will were conquering him and he were uneasy, but he held her eye with his own.

"You put me out to-night," he said.

"Yes, and I'm going to do it again. You're drunk."

She started to rise, but he took a step towards her and she paused. He looked as she had never seen him look before. His face was ashen and his eyes like fire and blood. She quailed beneath the look. He took another step towards her.

"You put me out to-night," he repeated, "like a dog."

His step was steady and his tone was clear, menacingly clear. She shrank back from him, back to the wall. Still his hands twitched and his eye held her. Still he crept slowly towards her, his lips working and his hands moving convulsively.

"Joe, Joe!" she said hoarsely, "what's the matter? Oh, don't look at me like that."

The gown had fallen away from her breast and showed the convulsive fluttering of her heart.

He broke into a laugh, a dry, murderous laugh, and his hands sought each other while the fingers twitched over one another like coiling serpents.

"You put me out—you—you, and you made me what I am." The realisation of what he was, of his foulness and degradation, seemed just to have come to him fully. "You made me what I am, and then you sent me away. You let me come back, and now you put me out."

She gazed at him, fascinated. She tried to scream and she could not. This was not Joe. This was not the boy that she had turned and twisted about her little finger. This was a terrible, terrible man or a monster.

He moved a step nearer her. His eyes fell to her throat. For an instant she lost their steady glare and then she found her voice. The scream was checked as it began. His fingers had closed over her throat just where the gown had left it temptingly bare. They gave it the caress of death. She struggled. They held her. Her eyes prayed to his. But his were the fire of hell. She fell back upon her pillow in silence. He had not uttered a word. He held her. Finally he flung her from him like a rag, and sank into a chair. And there the officers found him when Hattie Sterling's disappearance had become a strange thing.

CHAPTER 15

"Dear, Damned, Delightful Town"

WHEN JOE WAS TAKEN, there was no spirit or feeling left in him. He moved mechanically, as if without sense or volition. The first impression he gave was that of a man over-acting insanity. But this was soon removed by the very indifference with which he met everything concerned with his crime. From the very first he made no effort to exonerate or to vindicate himself. He talked little and only in a dry, stupefied way. He was as one whose soul is dead, and perhaps it was; for all the little soul of him had been wrapped up in the body of this one woman, and the stroke that took her life had killed him too.

The men who examined him were irritated beyond measure. There was nothing for them to exercise their ingenuity upon. He left them nothing to search for. Their most damning question he answered with an apathy that showed absolutely no interest in the matter. It was as if someone whom he did not care about had committed a crime and he had been called to testify. The only thing which he noticed or seemed to have any affection for was a little pet dog which had been hers and which they sometimes allowed to be with him after the life sentence had been passed upon him and when he was awaiting removal. He would sit for hours with the little animal in his lap, caressing it dumbly. There was a mute sorrow in the eyes of both man and dog, and they seemed to take comfort in each other's presence. There was no need of any sign between them. They had both loved her, had they not? So they understood.

Sadness saw him and came back to the Banner, torn and unnerved by the sight. "I saw him," he said with a shudder, "and it'll take more whiskey than Jack can give me in a year to wash the memory of him out of me. Why, man, it shocked me all through. It's a pity they didn't send him to the chair. It couldn't have done him much harm and would have been a real mercy."

And so Sadness and all the club, with a muttered "Poor devil!" dismissed him. He was gone. Why should they worry? Only one more who had got into the whirl-pool, enjoyed the sensation for a moment, and then swept dizzily down. There were, indeed, some who for an earnest hour sermonised about it and said, "Here is another example of the pernicious influence of the city on untrained negroes. Oh, is there no way to keep these people from rushing away from the small villages and country districts of the South up to the cities, where they cannot battle with the terrible force of a strange and unusual environment? Is there no way to prove to them that woollen-shirted, brown-jeaned simplicity is infinitely better than broad-clothed degradation?" They wanted to preach to these people that good agriculture is better than bad art,—that it was better and nobler for them to sing to God across the Southern fields than to dance for rowdies in the Northern halls. They wanted to dare to say that the South has its faults—no one con-dones them—and its disadvantages, but that even what they suffered from these was better than what awaited them in the great alleys of New York. Down there, the bodies were restrained, and they chafed; but here the soul would fester, and they would be content.

⌈This was but for an hour, for even while they exclaimed they knew that there was no way, and that the stream of young negro life would continue to flow up from the South, dashing itself against the hard necessities of the city and breaking like waves against a rock,—that, until the gods grew tired of their cruel sport, there must still be sacrifices to false ideals and unreal ambitions⌉

There was one heart, though, that neither dismissed Joe with gratuitous pity nor sermonised about him. The mother heart had only room for grief and pain. Already it had borne its share. It had known sorrow for a lost husband, tears at the neglect and brutality of a new companion, shame for a daughter's sake, and it had seemed already filled to overflowing. And yet the fates had put in this one other burden until it seemed it must burst with the weight of it.

To Fannie Hamilton's mind now all her boy's shortcomings became as naught. He was not her wayward, erring, criminal son. She only remembered that he was her son, and wept for him as such. She forgot his curses, while her memory went back to the sweetness of his baby prattle and the soft words of his tenderer youth. Until the last she clung to him, holding him guiltless, and to her thought they took to prison, not Joe Hamilton, a convicted criminal, but Joey, Joey, her boy, her firstborn,—a martyr.

The pretty Miss Kitty Hamilton was less deeply impressed. The arrest and subsequent conviction of her brother was quite a blow. She felt the shame of it keenly,

and some of the grief. To her, coming as it did just at a
time when the company was being strengthened and she
more importantly featured than ever, it was decidedly
inopportune, for no one could help connecting her name
with the affair.

For a long time she and her brother had scarcely been
upon speaking terms. During Joe's frequent lapses from
industry he had been prone to "touch" his sister for the
wherewithal to supply his various wants. When, finally,
she grew tired and refused to be "touched," he rebuked
her for withholding that which, save for his help, she
would never have been able to make. This went on until
they were almost entirely estranged. He was wont to say
that "now his sister was up in the world, she had got the
big head," and she to retort that her brother "wanted to
use her for a 'soft thing.'"

From the time that she went on the stage she had
begun to live her own life, a life in which the chief aim
was the possession of good clothes and the ability to attract the attention which she had learned to crave. The
greatest sign of interest she showed in her brother's affair was, at first, to offer her mother money to secure a
lawyer. But when Joe confessed all, she consoled herself
with the reflection that perhaps it was for the best, and
kept her money in her pocket with a sense of satisfaction. She was getting to be so very much more Joe's sister. She did not go to see her brother. She was afraid it
might make her nervous while she was in the city, and
she went on the road with her company before he was
taken away.

Miss Kitty Hamilton had to be very careful about her
nerves and her health. She had had experiences, and her
voice was not as good as it used to be, and her beauty

had to be aided by cosmetics. So she went away from New York, and only read of all that happened when some one called her attention to it in the papers.

Berry Hamilton in his Southern prison knew nothing of all this, for no letters had passed between him and his family for more than two years. The very cruelty of destiny defeated itself in this and was kind.

CHAPTER 16

Skaggs's Theory

THERE WAS, PERHAPS, more depth to Mr. Skaggs than most people gave him credit for having. However it may be, when he got an idea into his head, whether it were insane or otherwise, he had a decidedly tenacious way of holding to it. Sadness had been disposed to laugh at him when he announced that Joe's drunken story of his father's troubles had given him an idea. But it was, nevertheless, true, and that idea had stayed with him clear through the exciting events that followed on that fatal night. He thought and dreamed of it until he had made a working theory. Then one day, with a boldness that he seldom assumed when in the sacred Presence, he walked into the office and laid his plans before the editor. They talked together for some time, and the editor seemed hard to convince.

"It would be a big thing for the paper," he said, "if it only panned out; but it is such a rattle-brained, harum-scarum thing. No one under the sun would have thought of it but you, Skaggs."

"Oh, it's bound to pan out. I see the thing as clear as day. There's no getting around it."

"Yes, it looks plausible, but so does all fiction. You're taking a chance. You're losing time. If it fails——"

"But if it succeeds?"

"Well, go and bring back a story. If you don't, look out. It's against my better judgment anyway. Remember I told you that."

Skaggs shot out of the office, and within an hour and a half had boarded a fast train for the South.

It is almost a question whether Skaggs had a theory or whether he had told himself a pretty story and, as usual, believed it. The editor was right. No one else would have thought of the wild thing that was in the reporter's mind. The detective had not thought of it five years before, nor had Maurice Oakley and his friends had an inkling, and here was one of the New York *Universe*'s young men going miles to prove his idea about something that did not at all concern him.

When Skaggs reached the town which had been the home of the Hamiltons, he went at once to the Continental Hotel. He had as yet formulated no plan of immediate action and with a fool's or a genius's belief in his destiny he sat down to await the turn of events. His first move would be to get acquainted with some of his neighbours. This was no difficult matter, as the bar of the Continental was still the gathering-place of some of the city's choice spirits of the old régime. Thither he went, and his convivial cheerfulness soon placed him on terms of equality with many of his kind.

He insinuated that he was looking around for business prospects. This proved his open-sesame. Five years had not changed the Continental frequenters much, and Skaggs's intention immediately brought Beachfield Davis down upon him with the remark, "If a man wants to go into business, business for a gentleman, suh, Gad, there's no finer or better-paying business in the world than breeding blooded dogs—that is, if you get a man of experience to go in with you."

"Dogs, dogs," drivelled old Horace Talbot, "Beachfield's always talking about dogs. I remember the night we were all discussing that Hamilton nigger's arrest, Beachfield said it was a sign of total depravity because his man hunted 'possums with his hound." The old man laughed inanely. The hotel whiskey was getting on his nerves.

The reporter opened his eyes and his ears. He had stumbled upon something, at any rate.

"What was it about some nigger's arrest, sir?" he asked respectfully.

"Oh, it wasn't anything much. Only an old and trusted servant robbed his master, and my theory—"

"But you will remember, Mr. Talbot," broke in Davis, "that I proved your theory to be wrong and cited a conclusive instance."

"Yes, a 'possum-hunting dog."

"I am really anxious to hear about the robbery, though. It seems such an unusual thing for a negro to steal a great amount."

"Just so, and that was part of my theory. Now——"

"It's an old story and a long one, Mr. Skaggs, and one of merely local repute," interjected Colonel Saunders. "I don't think it could possibly interest you, who are familiar with the records of the really great crimes that take place in a city such as New York."

"Those things do interest me very much, though. I am something of a psychologist, and I often find the smallest and most insignificant-appearing details pregnant with suggestion. Won't you let me hear the story, Colonel?"

"Why, yes, though there's little in it save that I am one

of the few men who have come to believe that the negro, Berry Hamilton, is not the guilty party."

"Nonsense! nonsense!" said Talbot; "of course Berry was guilty, but, as I said before, I don't blame him. The negroes——"

"Total depravity," said Davis. "Now look at my dog——"

"If you will retire with me to the further table I will give you whatever of the facts I can call to mind."

As unobtrusively as they could, they drew apart from the others and seated themselves at a more secluded table, leaving Talbot and Davis wrangling, as of old, over their theories. When the glasses were filled and the pipes going, the Colonel began his story, interlarding it frequently with comments of his own.

"Now, in the first place, Mr. Skaggs," he said when the tale was done, "I am lawyer enough to see for myself how weak the evidence was upon which the negro was convicted, and later events have done much to confirm me in the opinion that he was innocent."

"Later events?"

"Yes." The Colonel leaned across the table and his voice fell to a whisper. "Four years ago a great change took place in Maurice Oakley. It happened in the space of a day, and no one knows the cause of it. From a social, companionable man, he became a recluse, shunning visitors and dreading society. From an open-hearted, unsuspicious neighbour, he became secretive and distrustful of his own friends. From an active business man, he has become a retired brooder. He sees no one if he can help it. He writes no letters and receives none, not even from his brother, it is said. And all of this came about in the space of twenty-four hours."

"But what was the beginning of it?"

"No one knows, save that one day he had some sort of nervous attack. By the time the doctor was called he was better, but he kept clutching his hand over his heart. Naturally, the physician wanted to examine him there, but the very suggestion of it seemed to throw him into a frenzy; and his wife too begged the doctor, an old friend of the family, to desist. Maurice Oakley had been as sound as a dollar, and no one of the family had had any tendency to heart affection."

"It is strange."

"Strange it is, but I have my theory."

"His actions are like those of a man guarding a secret."

"Sh! His negro laundress says that there is an inside pocket in his undershirts."

"An inside pocket?"

"Yes."

"And for what?" Skaggs was trembling with eagerness. The Colonel dropped his voice lower.

"We can only speculate," he said; "but, as I have said, I have my theory. Oakley was a just man, and in punishing his old servant for the supposed robbery it is plain that he acted from principle. But he is also a proud man and would hate to confess that he had been in the wrong. So I believe that the cause of his first shock was the finding of the money that he supposed gone. Unwilling to admit this error, he lets the misapprehension go on, and it is the money which he carries in his secret pocket, with a morbid fear of its discovery, that has made him dismiss his servants, leave his business, and refuse to see his friends."

"A very natural conclusion, Colonel, and I must say that I believe you. It is strange that others have not seen as you have seen and brought the matter to light."

"Well, you see, Mr. Skaggs, none are so dull as the

people who think they think. I can safely say that there is not another man in this town who has lighted upon the real solution of this matter, though it has been openly talked of for so long. But as for bringing it to light, no one would think of doing that. It would be sure to hurt Oakley's feelings, and he is of one of our best families."

"Ah, yes, perfectly right."

Skaggs had got all that he wanted; much more, in fact, than he had expected. The Colonel held him for a while yet to enlarge upon the views that he had expressed.

When the reporter finally left him, it was with a cheery "Good-night, Colonel. If I were a criminal, I should be afraid of that analytical mind of yours!"

He went upstairs chuckling. "The old fool!" he cried as he flung himself into a chair. "I've got it! I've got it! Maurice Oakley must see me, and then what?" He sat down to think out what he should do to-morrow. Again, with his fine disregard of ways and means, he determined to trust to luck, and as he expressed it, "brace old Oakley."

Accordingly he went about nine o'clock the next morning to Oakley's house. A gray-haired, sad-eyed woman inquired his errand.

"I want to see Mr. Oakley," he said.

"You cannot see him. Mr. Oakley is not well and does not see visitors."

"But I must see him, madam; I am here upon business of importance."

"You can tell me just as well as him. I am his wife and transact all of his business."

"I can tell no one but the master of the house himself."

"You cannot see him. It is against his orders."

"Very well," replied Skaggs, descending one step; "it is his loss, not mine. I have tried to do my duty and failed. Simply tell him that I came from Paris."

"Paris?" cried a querulous voice behind the woman's back. "Leslie, why do you keep the gentleman at the door? Let him come in at once."

Mrs. Oakley stepped from the door and Skaggs went in. Had he seen Oakley before he would have been shocked at the change in his appearance; but as it was, the nervous, white-haired man who stood shiftily before him told him nothing of an eating secret long carried. The man's face was gray and haggard, and deep lines were cut under his staring fish-like eyes. His hair tumbled in white masses over his pallid forehead, and his lips twitched as he talked.

"You're from Paris, sir, from Paris?" he said. "Come in, come in."

His motions were nervous and erratic. Skaggs followed him into the library, and the wife disappeared in another direction.

It would have been hard to recognize in the Oakley of the present the man of a few years before. The strong frame had gone away to bone, and nothing of his old power sat on either brow or chin. He was as a man who trembled on the brink of insanity. His guilty secret had been too much for him, and Skaggs's own fingers twitched as he saw his host's hands seek the breast of his jacket every other moment.

"It is there the secret is hidden," he said to himself, "and whatever it is, I must have it. But how—how? I can't knock the man down and rob him in his own house." But Oakley himself proceeded to give him his first cue.

"You—you—perhaps have a message from my brother—my brother who is in Paris. I have not heard from him for some time."

Skaggs's mind worked quickly. He remembered the Colonel's story. Evidently the brother had something to do with the secret. "Now or never," he thought. So he said boldly, "Yes, I have a message from your brother."

The man sprung up, clutching again at his breast. "You have? you have? Give it to me. After four years he sends me a message! Give it to me!"

The reporter looked steadily at the man. He knew that he was in his power, that his very eagerness would prove traitor to his discretion.

"Your brother bade me to say to you that you have a terrible secret, that you bear it in your breast—there—there. I am his messenger. He bids you to give it to me."

Oakley had shrunken back as if he had been struck.

"No, no!" he gasped, "no, no! I have no secret."

The reporter moved nearer him. The old man shrank against the wall, his lips working convulsively and his hand tearing at his breast as Skaggs drew nearer. He attempted to shriek, but his voice was husky and broke off in a gasping whisper.

"Give it to me, as your brother commands."

"No, no, no! It is not his secret; it is mine. I must carry it here always—do you hear? I must carry it till I die. Go away! Go away!"

Skaggs seized him. Oakley struggled weakly, but he had no strength. The reporter's hand sought the secret pocket. He felt a paper beneath his fingers. Oakley gasped hoarsely as he drew it forth. Then raising his voice gave one agonized cry, and sank to the floor, frothing at the mouth. At the cry rapid footsteps were heard in the hallway, and Mrs. Oakley threw open the door.

"What is the matter?" she cried.

"My message has somewhat upset your husband," was the cool answer.

"But his breast is open. Your hand has been in his

bosom. You have taken something from him. Give it to me, or I shall call for help."

Skaggs had not reckoned on this, but his wits came to the rescue.

"You dare not call for help," he said, "or the world will know!"

She wrung her hands helplessly, crying, "Oh, give it to me, give it to me. We've never done you any harm."

"But you've harmed someone else; that is enough."

He moved towards the door, but she sprang in front of him with the fierceness of a tigress protecting her young. She attacked him with teeth and nails. She was pallid with fury, and it was all he could do to protect himself and yet not injure her. Finally, when her anger had taken her strength, he succeeded in getting out. He flew down the hallway and out of the front door, the woman's screams following him. He did not pause to read the precious letter until he was safe in his room at the Continental Hotel. Then he sprang to his feet, crying, "Thank God! thank God! I was right, and the *Universe* shall have a sensation. The brother is the thief, and Berry Hamilton is an innocent man. Hurrah! Now, who is it that has come on a wild-goose chase? Who is it that ought to handle his idea carefully? Heigho, Saunders, my man, the drinks'll be on you, and old Skaggsy will have done some good in the world."

CHAPTER 17

A Yellow Journal

MR. SKAGGS HAD no qualms of conscience about the manner in which he had come by the damaging evidence against Maurice Oakley. It was enough for him that he had it. A corporation, he argued, had no soul, and therefore no conscience. How much less, then, should so small a part of a great corporation as himself be expected to have them?

He had his story. It was vivid, interesting, dramatic. It meant the favour of his editor, a big thing for the *Universe,* and a fatter lining for his own pocket. He sat down to put his discovery on paper before he attempted anything else, although the impulse to celebrate was very strong within him.

He told his story well, with an eye to every one of its salient points. He sent an alleged picture of Berry Hamilton as he had appeared at the time of his arrest. He sent a picture of the Oakley home and of the cottage where the servant and his family had been so happy. There was a strong pen-picture of the man, Oakley, grown haggard and morose from carrying his guilty secret, of his confusion when confronted with the supposed knowledge of it. The old Southern city was described, and the opinions of its residents in regard to the case given. It was there—clear, interesting, and strong. One could see it all as if every phase of it were being enacted before one's eyes. Skaggs surpassed himself.

When the editor first got hold of it he said "Huh!" over the opening lines,—a few short sentences that instantly pricked the attention awake. He read on with increasing interest. "This is good stuff," he said at the last page. "Here's a chance for the *Universe* to look into the methods of Southern court proceedings. Here's a chance for a spread."

The *Universe* had always claimed to be the friend of all poor and oppressed humanity, and every once in a while it did something to substantiate its claim, whereupon it stood off and said to the public, "Look you what we have done, and behold how great we are, the friend of the people!" The *Universe* was yellow. It was very so. But it had power and keenness and energy. It never lost an opportunity to crow, and if one was not forthcoming, it made one. In this way it managed to do a considerable amount of good, and its yellowness became forgivable, even commendable. In Skaggs's story the editor saw an opportunity for one of its periodical philanthropies. He seized upon it. With headlines that took half a page, and with cuts authentic and otherwise, the tale was told, and the people of New York were greeted next morning with the announcement of—

> "A BURNING SHAME!
> A POOR AND INNOCENT NEGRO
> MADE TO SUFFER
> FOR A RICH MAN'S CRIME!

GREAT EXPOSÉ BY THE 'UNIVERSE'!
A 'UNIVERSE' REPORTER TO THE RESCUE!
THE WHOLE THING TO BE AIRED THAT THE
PEOPLE MAY KNOW!"

Then Skaggs received a telegram that made him leap for joy. He was to do it. He was to go to the capital of the State. He was to beard the Governor in his den, and he, with the force of a great paper behind him, was to demand for the people the release of an innocent man. Then there would be another write-up and much glory for him and more shekels. In an hour after he had received his telegram he was on his way to the Southern capital.

Meanwhile in the house of Maurice Oakley there were sad times. From the moment that the master of the house had fallen to the floor in impotent fear and madness there had been no peace within his doors. At first his wife had tried to control him alone, and had humoured the wild babblings with which he woke from his swoon. But these changed to shrieks and cries and curses, and she was forced to throw open the doors so long closed and call in help. The neighbours and her old friends went to her assistance, and what the reporter's story had not done, the ravings of the man accomplished; for, with a show of matchless cunning, he continually clutched at his breast, laughed, and babbled his secret openly. Even then they would have smothered it in silence, for the honour of one of their best families; but too many ears had heard, and then came the yellow journal bearing all the news in emblazoned headlines.

Colonel Saunders was distinctly hurt to think that his

confidence had been imposed on, and that he had been instrumental in bringing shame upon a Southern name.

"To think, suh," he said generally to the usual assembly of choice spirits,—"to think of that man's being a reporter, such a common, ordinary reporter, and that I sat and talked to him as if he were a gentleman!"

"You're not to be blamed, Colonel," said old Horace Talbot. "You've done no more than any other gentleman would have done. The trouble is that the average Northerner has no sense of honour, suh, no sense of honour. If this particular man had had, he would have kept still, and everything would have gone on smooth and quiet. Instead of that, a distinguished family is brought to shame, and for what? To give a nigger a few more years of freedom when, likely as not, he don't want it; and Berry Hamilton's life in prison has proved nearer the ideal reached by slavery than anything he has found since emancipation. Why, suhs, I fancy I see him leaving his prison with tears of regret in his eyes."

Old Horace was inanely eloquent for an hour over his pet theory. But there were some in the town who thought differently about the matter, and it was their opinions and murmurings that backed up Skaggs and made it easier for him when at the capital he came into contact with the official red tape.

He was told that there were certain forms of procedure, and certain times for certain things, but he hammered persistently away, the murmurings behind him grew louder, while from his sanctum the editor of the *Universe* thundered away against oppression and high-handed tyranny. Other papers took it up and asked why this man should be despoiled of his liberty any longer? And when it was replied that the man had been convicted, and that the wheels of justice could not be stopped or turned back by the letter of a romantic artist or the ravings of a madman, there was a mighty outcry against the farce of justice that had been played out in this man's case.

The trial was reviewed; the evidence again brought up and examined. The dignity of the State was threatened. At this time the State did the one thing necessary to save its tottering reputation. It would not surrender, but it capitulated, and Berry Hamilton was pardoned.

Berry heard the news with surprise and a half-bitter joy. He had long ago lost hope that justice would ever be done to him. He marvelled at the word that was brought to him now, and he could not understand the strange cordiality of the young white man who met him at the warden's office. Five years of prison life had made a different man of him. He no longer looked to receive kindness from his fellows, and he blinked at it as he blinked at the unwonted brightness of the sun. The lines about his mouth where the smiles used to gather had changed and grown stern with the hopelessness of years. His lips drooped pathetically, and hard treatment had given his eyes a lowering look. His hair, that had hardly shown a white streak, was as white as Maurice Oakley's own. His erstwhile quick wits were dulled and imbruted. He had lived like an ox, working without inspiration or reward, and he came forth like an ox from his stall. All the higher part of him he had left behind, dropping it off day after day through the wearisome years. He had put behind him the Berry Hamilton that laughed and joked and sang and believed, for even his faith had become only a numbed fancy.

"This is a very happy occasion, Mr. Hamilton," said Skaggs, shaking his hand heartily.

Berry did not answer. What had this slim, glib young man to do with him? What had any white man to do with him after what he had suffered at their hands?

"You know you are to go to New York with me?"

"To New Yawk? What fu'?"

Skaggs did not tell him that, now that the *Universe* had done its work, it demanded the right to crow to its heart's satisfaction. He said only, "You want to see your wife, of course?"

Berry had forgotten Fannie, and for the first time his heart thrilled within him at the thought of seeing her again.

"I ain't hyeahed f'om my people fu' a long time. I didn't know what had become of 'em. How's Kit an' Joe?"

"They're all right," was the reply. Skaggs couldn't tell him, in this the first hour of his freedom. Let him have time to drink the sweetness of that all in. There would be time afterwards to taste all of the bitterness.

Once in New York, he found that people wished to see him, some fools, some philanthropists, and a great many reporters. He had to be photographed—all this before he could seek those whom he longed to see. They printed his picture as he was before he went to prison and as he was now, a sort of before-and-after-taking comment, and in the morning that it all appeared, when the *Universe* spread itself to tell the public what it had done and how it had done it, they gave him his wife's address.

It would be better, they thought, for her to tell him herself all that happened. No one of them was brave enough to stand to look in his eyes when he asked for his son and daughter, and they shifted their responsibility by pretending to themselves that they were doing it for his own good: that the blow would fall more gently upon him coming from her who had been his wife. Berry took the address and inquired his way timidly, hesitatingly, but with a swelling heart, to the door of the flat where Fannie lived.

CHAPTER 18

What Berry Found

HAD NOT BERRY'S years of prison life made him forget what little he knew of reading, he might have read the name Gibson on the door-plate where they told him to ring for his wife. But he knew nothing of what awaited him as he confidently pulled the bell. Fannie herself came to the door. The news the papers held had not escaped her, but she had suffered in silence, hoping that Berry might be spared the pain of finding her. Now he stood before her, and she knew him at a glance, in spite of his haggard countenance.

"Fannie," he said, holding out his arms to her, and all of the pain and pathos of long yearning was in his voice, "don't you know me?"

She shrank away from him, back in the hall-way.

"Yes, yes, Be'y, I knows you. Come in."

She led him through the passage-way and into her room, he following with a sudden sinking at his heart. This was not the reception he had expected from Fannie.

When they were within the room he turned and held out his arms to her again, but she did not notice them. "Why, is you 'shamed o' me?" he asked brokenly.

" 'Shamed? No! Oh, Be'y," and she sank into a chair and began rocking to and fro in her helpless grief.

"What's de mattah, Fannie? Ain't you glad to see me?"

"Yes, yes, but you don't know nothin', do you? Dey lef' me to tell you?"

"Lef' you to tell me? What's de mattah? Is Joe or Kit daid? Tell me."

"No, not daid. Kit dances on de stage fu' a livin', an', Be'y, she ain't de gal she ust to be. Joe—Joe—Joe—he's in pen'tentiary fu' killin' a ooman."

Berry started forward with a cry, "My Gawd! my Gawd! my little gal! my boy!"

"Dat ain't all," she went on dully, as if reciting a rote lesson; "I ain't yo' wife no mo'. I's ma'ied ag'in. Oh, Be'y, Be'y, don't look at me lak dat. I couldn't he'p it. Kit an' Joe lef' me, an' dey said de pen'tentiary divo'ced you an' me, an' dat you'd nevah come out nohow. Don't look at me lak dat, Be'y."

"You ain't my wife no mo'? Hit's a lie, a damn lie! You is my wife. I's a innocent man. No pen'tentiary kin tek you erway f'om me. Hit's enough what dey've done to my chillen." He rushed forward and seized her by the arm. "Dey sha'n't do no mo', by Gawd! dey sha'n't, I say!" His voice had risen to a fierce roar, like that of a hurt beast, and he shook her by the arm as he spoke.

"Oh, don't, Be'y, don't. You hu't me. I couldn't he'p it."

He glared at her for a moment, and then the real force of the situation came full upon him, and he bowed his head in his hands and wept like a child. The great sobs came up and stuck in his throat.

She crept up to him fearfully and laid her hand on his head.

"Don't cry, Be'y," she said; "I done wrong, but I loves you yit."

He seized her in his arms and held her tightly until he could control himself. Then he asked weakly, "Well, what am I goin' to do?"

"I do' know, Be'y, 'ceptin' dat you'll have to leave me."

"I won't! I'll never leave you again," he replied doggedly.

"But, Be'y, you mus'. You'll only mek it ha'der on me, an' Gibson'll beat me ag'in."

"Ag'in!"

She hung her head: "Yes."

He gripped himself hard.

"Why cain't you come on off wid me, Fannie? You was mine fus'."

"I couldn't. He would fin' me anywhaih I went to."

"Let him fin' you. You'll be wid me, an' we'll settle it, him an' me."

"I want to, but oh, I can't, I can't," she wailed. "Please go now, Be'y, befo' he gits home. He's mad anyhow, 'cause you're out."

Berry looked at her hard, and then said in a dry voice, "An' so I got to go an' leave you to him?"

"Yes, you mus'; I'm his'n now."

He turned to the door, murmuring, "My wife gone, Kit a nobody, an' Joe, little Joe, a murderer, an' then I—I—ust to pray to Gawd an' call him 'Ouah Fathah.'" He laughed hoarsely. It sounded like nothing Fannie had ever heard before.

"Don't, Be'y, don't say dat. Maybe we don't un'erstan'."

Her faith still hung by a slender thread, but his had given way in that moment.

"No, we don't un'erstan'," he laughed as he went out of the door. "We don't un'erstan'."

He staggered down the steps, blinded by his emotions, and set his face towards the little lodging that he had taken temporarily. There seemed nothing left in life for him to do. Yet he knew that he must work to live, although the effort seemed hardly worth while. He remembered now that the *Universe* had offered him the under janitorship in its building. He would go and take it, and some day, perhaps— He was not quite sure what the "perhaps" meant. But as his mind grew clearer he came to know, for a sullen, fierce anger was smoldering in his heart against the man who through lies had stolen his wife from him. It was anger that came slowly, but gained in fierceness as it grew.

Yes, that was it—he would kill Gibson. It was no worse than his present state. Then it would be father and son murderers. They would hang him or send him back to prison. Neither would be hard now. He laughed to himself.

And this was what they had let him out of prison for? To find out all this. Why had they not left him there to die in ignorance? What had he to do with all these people who gave him sympathy? What did he want of their sympathy? Could they give him back one tithe of what he had lost? Could they restore to him his wife or his son or his daughter, his quiet happiness or his simple faith?

He went to work for the *Universe,* but night after night, armed, he patrolled the sidewalk in front of Fannie's house. He did not know Gibson, but he wanted to see them together. Then he would strike. His vigils kept him from his bed, but he went to the next morning's work with no weariness. The hope of revenge sustained him, and he took a savage joy in the thought that he should be the dispenser of justice to at least one of those who had wounded him.

Finally he grew impatient and determined to wait no longer, but to seek his enemy in his own house. He approached the place cautiously and went up the steps. His hand touched the bell-pull. He staggered back.

"Oh, my Gawd!" he said.

There was crape on Fannie's bell. His head went round and he held to the door for support. Then he turned the knob and the door opened. He went noiselessly in. At the door of Fannie's room he halted, sick with fear. He knocked, a step sounded within, and his wife's face looked out upon him. He could have screamed aloud with relief.

"It ain't you!" he whispered huskily.

"No, it's him. He was killed in a fight at the racetrack. Some o' his friends are settin' up. Come in."

He went in, a wild, strange feeling surging at his heart. She showed him into the death-chamber.

As he stood and looked down upon the face of his enemy, still, cold, and terrible in death, the recognition of how near he had come to crime swept over him, and all his dead faith sprang into new life in a glorious resurrection. He stood with clasped hands, and no word passed his lips. But his heart was crying, "Thank God! thank God! this man's blood is not on my hands."

The gamblers who were sitting up with the dead wondered who the old fool was who looked at their silent comrade and then raised his eyes as if in prayer.

When Gibson was laid away, there were no formalities between Berry and his wife; they simply went back to each other. New York held nothing for them now but sad memories. Kit was on the road, and the father could not bear to see his son; so they turned their faces southward, back to the only place they could call home. Surely the people could not be cruel to them now, and even if they were, they felt that after what they had endured no wound had power to give them pain.

Leslie Oakley heard of their coming, and with her own hands reopened and refurnished the little cottage in the yard for them. There the white-haired woman begged them to spend the rest of their days and be in peace and comfort. It was the only amend she could make. As much to satisfy her as to settle themselves, they took the cottage, and many a night thereafter they sat together with clasped hands, listening to the shrieks of the madman across the yard and thinking of what he had brought to them and to himself.

It was not a happy life, but it was all that was left to them, and they took it up without complaint, for they knew they were powerless against some Will infinitely stronger than their own.

yikes

Selected Bibliography

Works by Paul Laurence Dunbar

Poetry

Oak and Ivy, 1893
Majors and Minors, 1895
Lyrics of a Lowly Life, 1896
Lyrics of a Hearthside, 1899
Poems of Cabin and Field, 1899
Candle-Lightin' Time, 1901
Lyrics of Love and Laughter, 1903
When Malindy Sings, 1903
Li'l Gal, 1904
Chris'mus Is a Comin', and Other Poems, 1905
Howdy, Honey, Howdy, 1905
Lyrics of Sunshine and Shadow, 1905
A Plantation Portrait, 1905
Joggin' Erlong, 1906

Fiction

Folks from Dixie, 1898 Stories
The Uncalled, 1898 Novel
The Strength of Gideon and Other Stories, 1900 Stories
The Love of Landry, 1900 Novel

The Fanatics, 1901 Novel
The Sport of the Gods, 1902 Novel
In Old Plantation Days, 1903 Stories
The Heart of the Happy Hollow, 1904 Stories

Biography and Criticism

Alexander, Eleanor. *Lyrics of Sunshine and Shadow: The Tragic Courtship and Marriage of Paul Laurence Dunbar*. New York: New York University Press, 2001.

Best, Felton O. *Crossing the Color Line: A Biography of Paul Laurence Dunbar*. Dubuque, IA: Kendall/Hunt, 1996.

Gayle, Addison, Jr. *Oak and Ivy: A Biography of Paul Laurence Dunbar*. New York: Doubleday, 1971.

Hudson, Gossie Harold. *A Biography of Paul Laurence Dunbar*. Baltimore, MD: Gateway, 1999.

Hudson, Gossie H. and Jay Martin, eds. *The Paul Laurence Dunbar Reader: A Selection of the Best of Paul Laurence Dunbar's Poetry and Prose, Including Writings Never Before Available in Book Form*. New York: Dodd, Mead, & Co., 1975.

Martin, Herbert W. and Ronald Primeau, eds. *In His Own Voice: The Dramatic and Other Uncollected Works of Paul Laurence Dunbar*. Athens, OH: Ohio University Press, 2002.

Martin, Jay, ed. *A Singer in the Dawn: Reinterpretations of Paul Laurence Dunbar*. New York: Dodd, Mead, & Co., 1975.

Revell, Peter. *Paul Laurence Dunbar*. Boston, MA: Twayne, 1979.

Wagner, Jean. *Black Poets of the United States: From Paul Laurence Dunbar to Langston Hughes*. Champaign: University of Illinois Press, 1973.

Thought-Provoking Essays

WHY WE CAN'T WAIT
by Reverend Martin Luther King, Jr.
Here are King's explanations of the events, forces, and
pressures behind the quest for and necessity of equality
guaranteed by civil rights under the law for all Americans.
Contains the seminal Letter from Birmingham Jail.

TO BE YOUNG, GIFTED AND BLACK
by Lorraine Hansberry
The author of *A Raisin in the Sun* tells of her early life
as a writer in an artistic world dominated and
controlled by whites.

BLACK LIKE ME
by John Howard Griffin
The chilling odyssey through the Deep South of a
white man who disguised himself as a black man, in
order to better understand the conditions of blacks in
America in the early 1960s.

S486

READ THE TOP 20
SIGNET CLASSICS

ANIMAL FARM BY GEORGE ORWELL

1984 BY GEORGE ORWELL

NARRATIVE OF THE LIFE OF FREDERICK DOUGLASS
   BY FREDERICK DOUGLASS

BEOWULF (BURTON RAFFEL, TRANSLATOR)

FRANKENSTEIN BY MARY SHELLEY

ALICE'S ADVENTURES IN WONDERLAND &
   THROUGH THE LOOKING GLASS BY LEWIS CARROLL

THE INFERNO BY DANTE

COMMON SENSE, RIGHTS OF MAN, AND OTHER
   ESSENTIAL WRITINGS BY THOMAS PAINE

HAMLET BY WILLIAM SHAKESPEARE

A TALE OF TWO CITIES BY CHARLES DICKENS

THE HUNCHBACK OF NOTRE DAME BY VICTOR HUGO

THE FEDERALIST PAPERS BY ALEXANDER HAMILTON

THE SCARLET LETTER BY NATHANIEL HAWTHORNE

DRACULA BY BRAM STOKER

THE HOUND OF THE BASKERVILLES
   BY SIR ARTHUR CONAN DOYLE

WUTHERING HEIGHTS BY EMILY BRONTË

THE ODYSSEY BY HOMER

A MIDSUMMER NIGHT'S DREAM BY WILLIAM SHAKESPEARE

FRANKENSTEIN; DRACULA; DR. JEKYLL AND MR. HYDE
   BY MARY SHELLEY, BRAM STOKER, AND ROBERT LOUIS STEVENSON

THE CLASSIC SLAVE NARRATIVES
   EDITED BY HENRY LOUIS GATES, JR.